Seven Seeds of Summer

Chantal Gadoury

Published by Waldorf Publishing
2140 Hall Johnson Road
#102-345
Grapevine, Texas 76051
www.WaldorfPublishing.com

Seven Seeds of Summer
ISBN: 978-1-944247-03-4
Library of Congress: 2015958878
Copyright © 2016

Dedication

To my Mom, my Dad, my Sister and to Roberto – Without any of you, this novel would not be what it is.
I love all of you.

Chapter One

"Summer!"

I could hear my friend, Maggie shouting my name across campus. There wasn't one person who hadn't heard my name. My cheeks heated with my embarrassment, and I slowly turned to see Maggie running toward me. Her brown hair billowing in her face as her loose ponytail fell apart. I caught myself grinning at seeing her dressed in her paint-splotched overalls again. She was always adamant that they were her lucky painting clothes. It was all I ever saw Maggie wear to classes. She advertised "artist."

"Hey Maggie," I murmured, giving her a small smile. I clung to my oversized sketchbook and waited for her to catch her breath.

"Are you going home now?" she asked me, pushing her hands on her waist, looking as if it was all she could do to hold herself up, either from the all-nighter that she more than likely had in finishing her project, or the fatigue in wrapping up the semester and packing to go home. I gave her a curt nod and turned my head in the direction of my mother, seeing her stuffing one of the last boxes from my dorm room into her car. Spring semester was finally over, and I was officially considered a sophomore in college. Thank God. No more "annoying freshman" classification.

"Aw, that's too bad. A bunch of us from Sketch class were going to head over to Rusty's Grill for a goodbye lunch," she said as she pushed her bangs from her face. I noticed her hands were still dirty from painting. I wondered how long she had been in the studio overnight working on the last project of the year – the one due this morning. I let out a sigh and shrugged.

"I'm sorry, Maggie. My mom and I have a long drive," I glanced over in my mother's direction again. She was standing by the car with her arms folded across her chest, expectantly looking at Maggie and me. "I better get going. I'm sorry for leaving in such a rush. I'll keep in touch with you over the summer." I lied as best as I could. It was hard to walk away from a person that only wanted to be my friend. I just didn't want any friends. I had spent the entire year in the studio, painting, drawing, painting, and drawing. Lunch and dinners usually consisted of me, alone; grabbing something from the Quick-Fix in the student center and taking it to my dorm room. Usually, that was the only time my roommate saw me. I must have made Rachel's life very easy.

For the next year, I applied for a single, so I could set up my easel and paint into the wee hours of the morning and not have to worry about bothering someone with the stenches of paint, or the tiny trickle of classical music escaping from my computer.

"Who was that?" my mother asked me as we climbed into her silver 1990 Honda Accord.

"That was just Maggie," I murmured, pushing my pillow towards my feet as I reached for my seat belt. "She was in a few of my art classes with me." I clicked the seat belt into place and pulled the pillow back up into my lap.

"You never mentioned a Maggie," my mother said, glancing over her shoulder as she backed out of the parking lot and started to drive toward the exit of the Institute.

"I never had to mention a Maggie," I said, pushing my pillow against the window and leaning on it. I knew what was coming next. My mother was going to tell me how much she wished I had made friends at school, and if I applied myself more, I would be happier. In her mind, not so alone, but I enjoyed being alone, for the most part.

"Honey, I think friends would be something positive in your life. You need friends. You always do everything alone. Every time either your father or I would call you, you were always alone. Always in the studio. Always doing something. You never even tried to be friends with your roommate."

"You don't know that!" I growled and closed my eyes, wanting her to drop it.

"I do know it, Summer. If you just tried hard enough, you could be so much happier. You have so much potential to do so many great things, and meet people. If you don't try hard, you'll never have those opportunities."

"I don't want friends, Mom. I just want my art degree and to move on, get a job and live."

"But you are living," she argued. "What do you think you're doing now? This is life, honey. This is it. We didn't just fork over the money to The New England Art Institute for you to just sit in a studio…"

"I thought you were paying for my education. For my future, to get a great job in something I love to do. Not make friends."

"We thought this place would open you up, and give you a chance to test your social skills."

"I've been weighed and measured, and ta-dah, I have none," I said using my favorite quote from one of my favorite movies.

"You don't have to be so negative all the time," my mother sighed, pushing her sunglasses over her eyes.

I could tell this was going to be a long drive. The New England Art Institute was only an hour away from Point Judith, where we lived in a small house by the ocean. It was probably my favorite place in the whole world. There was nothing but ocean, and sand and more opportunities to paint quietly.

"Your father is back in Greece," my mother murmured after a few minutes of nothing but the silence and the soft hum of the air conditioner.

"Again?" I asked, opening my eyes to glance at her. She nodded, not looking away from the road. "He was called out about three days ago. They found something more on the Hades location."

"Elis?"

"Yes," she said with a grin. "Elis."

"They found something more than rock and rubble?"

"Well, they just asked your father to come out and give his opinion on their recent findings. I'm not even sure what exactly they wanted him to look at."

"Rock and rubble," I finished, lowering my head back down onto my pillow. My family loved anything that had to do with Greek Mythology. Our house was filled with relics, and pictures of relics, statues, and temples. My mother was fascinated by Aphrodite, the Goddess of Love. I was sure it was because my mother was in love with the idea of love. She lived for Valentine's Day and stories of

Cupid and was fascinated by how love worked in strangers lives. It could have been the fact that she was a psychologist and loved studying people, but I had a feeling the reasons for her fascination delved much deeper than what surfaced.

There were pictures that littered our fridge and our hallways of my parents in their younger years, posing in front of all sorts of different temples. I imagine this is where or why my mother began her fascination with the Greek Gods and Goddesses. It must have started out as just an admiration until she started to pray to them. The only part of her decision to pray to them that bothered her was my growing adoration for Hades through my childhood, into my adolescent years. I had the freedom to explore and learn more about my dark friend, and even at times, prayed to him in the quietness of my mind.

I started at a very young age, after being told of the story of Hades and his love, Persephone. In my eyes, he was the perfect man. I became obsessed with him.

"Do you have to be so morbid?" my mother asked me when I told her of my fascination in our kitchen one morning. "Can't you choose another God to like?"

"Why should I have to? You can't make fun of me for liking him when you decided against going to church like all the other normal families," I asked, hoping I'd make my point with her.

"Normal is over-rated, honey. Don't be ashamed to be different."

"Then I'll stick with Hades," I said, giving her a smile. "He's different, and I like him."

It could have been the story that I heard growing up as a child. It could have even been the Disney version of Hercules when Hades was given blue hair that started my admiration for him. I always felt a tug toward him that I couldn't understand. There were several paintings that littered my room, filled with black oil paint and faces that longed for love and daylight. He was something that I had created in my imagination, and I desperately wanted for him to be alive and real.

But I knew they were only stories.

"Why do you like him so much?" my mother asked me one evening when she came into my room and caught me painting his dark face. He was a mix of colors; all washed in water and coal dust. He was my perfect creation.

"I feel like he knows me," I uttered, lost in the painting, washing his eyes with a blue paint that seemed to encase the loneliness that I knew he suffered. In those dark caverns, filled with spirits and doom, I knew that my God wanted to have more than what he already knew. He wanted to taste love and companionship. When I looked up, I saw my mother giving me a weird look, and I knew I needed to explain and find the words to describe the connection that I felt.

"I don't know, Mom. I guess it's like that God-human connection people get with Jesus."

"Jesus and Hades are two very different people, Summer," my mother said in a stern voice.

"Well, yeah. Hades is a God," I said with a smile.

"I don't think your obsession is healthy."

"I'm not obsessed, and I'm not worshipping him or anything."

"What do you call that?" She pointed to my painting in front of me. My hands were all black from the watercolor when I glanced at my work. "Or that?" she said when she pointed to the collection of other paintings leaning against the wall near my bed; my dark love.

"A creative outlet," I said with a smile.

"You need to let that go," she said, shaking her head.

"Why do I have to let it go? He's not a bad person or anything," I argued.

"He's the God of the Underworld, Summer. Don't you think that classifies him as a bad person?"

I shook my head and lowered my brush onto my desk and lifted the half-painted drawing to show her. "He didn't choose the Underworld, Mom. If you remember right, Zeus took the Universe, Poseidon chose the oceans, and that only left Hades with the Underworld."

"I already know the story, Summer," she murmured, leaning her body against my door.

"He's not really a villain at all. He's just the keeper of souls. Without death, there can be no life," I said, trying to defend him.

"You really need to find a new hobby Summer, or a new God to fantasize about."

"Why should I? You're the one that worships all of them. I just love one."

"I don't make my whole life about them."

I lowered the painting back down onto my desk and shook my head. "Yes, you do. Have you taken a look at our house? They're everywhere. You and Dad have made this house into a temple of your own."

"And you've made your room into a temple for Hades. How do you think that looks to us?" she shouted, lifting her hands into her hair. I could tell that she was frustrated and was about to "let me have it." My mother made accusations that she was going to "Let me have it one day." Maybe today would be that day.

"Dad doesn't think that," I argued back.

"You don't know what your father thinks about you," she accused as she closed the door behind her in disgust; her disgust echoed all around me.

"I guess that leaves the two of us," I whispered, glancing back down at my painting.

My dad was more willing to understand. He loved all the Gods – loved learning about ancient Greek culture, and mythology. He loved Apollo and Hermes; probably more so because he could relate to what they were Gods of.

"What do you think that says about me?" my dad asked one evening while we were driving back home from one of his Greek artifacts exhibits. We had all been comparing Gods and Goddesses, and I was extra careful not to ruin the conversation with any mention of Hades.

"That you like order and being the middleman to everyone," my mother said with a smile. I saw my father wink at my mother under the orange glow of the highway streetlights. It was true. My dad often played the middleman in between my mother and me in fights. He was usually the only reason why we made up. There had been plenty of nights when my father came into my room and tried to apologize on my mom's behalf, or beckoned me to come to their room to talk to her. He'd sit on the edge of the bed and coax me out with stories of Greece, of his childhood, and sometimes even with stories of the Gods and Goddesses that he claimed no one knew about. I had always suspected that there was more to them than what was written in countless books, and my dad was the only clever man who knew about them.

My attention snapped back to the present, as I thought of something. "Do you know when Dad will be back from Greece?" I asked my mom, as she drove past the "Welcome to Point Judith" sign.

Point Judith was a small town at the southern-most point of Rhode Island. It was beautiful; the kind of beauty that you find on postcards with tall, white lighthouses and lobster boats. It was a quiet place. The only sounds at night were of dinging bells on the buoys and the silent waves that crashed onto the white, powdery beaches. I couldn't wait to pull my shoes off and walk around in the cool evening sand.

"He's going to be there for a few more days. He'll be back Wednesday night." It was only Friday. I did the math, counting down the days in my mind. That meant Saturday, Sunday, Monday and Tuesday alone with my mom. I anticipated it would be a long couple of days. Days filled with my mom trying to do things with me, while I'd try and escape; searching to do anything other than what she'd plan. She liked to go into town and look at other peoples gardens. She liked to go to farm festivals, if she could ever find one near the shore and spend hours looking at their fresh produce and greens, commenting on how well or poor their harvest had been. I'd count the hours on my wristwatch, hoping for some relief in the hours to come. Just as all mothers seemed to do, from what I observed

9

from the few tourists that trekked to Point Judith, and from the high school classmates, my mother was notorious for pulling me around, station to station, talking about my schooling, the things that I was doing, and the things that she hoped I'd do in the coming years. She wanted what was best for me - a good education and a good head on my shoulders to face the world with once I was done with school. I wanted to focus on the few more years I had before I had to face those realities. The only highlight was the promise in the coming days for me: the chance to run away after dinner to the shore, and spend the last few hours of daylight lost in the strokes of my paintbrushes, the colors of the night sky and the images of faces and scenes in my mind.

"What do you want for dinner?" my mother eyed the local McDonalds as we slowly drove past it. I already knew she wanted to stop there and eat, and not have to be bothered to cook anything when we got back to the house. She hated to cook. She'd much rather be out in her gardens planting and weeding, than being bothered to take the meat out of the freezer and prepare it and have to plan side dishes and desserts. She'd rather pay for someone else to do it for her. There was a joke that if my father ever died, my mother and I would most likely starve if there was no such thing as take-out or drive-thru's.

"Dad didn't leave you any TV dinners in the freezer?" I asked, amused. She gave me a small smile and shook her head. "I've been eating them for the past two days. I think I could use some real grease in my system." My mother didn't hesitate to make the decision for me. She pulled into

the U-Turn lane and went back to her favorite grease-filled
fast food stop.

Chapter Two

After my mother got her fix with French fries, a hamburger, and a coke, we were on our way home to empty out the car.

When my mother pulled into our long gravel driveway, I could see the ghost of our house standing in the night. It felt like months had passed since I'd last seen my house, and my fingers itched for the door latch.

The moment my mother turned off the ignition, I pushed the car door open, and the ocean breeze was on my face. It carried the very ocean scent that took me back to my childhood; building sandcastles with our Old English sheepdog, Max, named cleverly after a favorite fairy tale of mine. There had been times that I couldn't sleep and opened my window and listened to the quiet bell on the buoy coming from the ocean – the silent lullaby I heard every time I started to paint on the shore.

"Welcome home." My mother laughed as she watched my expression. I gave her a smile as I grabbed the boxes from the back seat. Thank God I already mailed home most of my belongings. I knew that not all of it would fit into my mom's small Honda. She grabbed a box and followed me into the house, where bursts of color greeted me in our living room. My paintings of the ocean were on the wall.

"You hung my paintings?" I asked in shock, lowering the boxes onto the floor next to the door. I saw my mother nod as she eyed the painting of the landscape of the ocean; my favorite one.

"I hung the ones that didn't include *him*," she murmured, giving me the eye. The eye was the look of annoyance. Her dislike for Hades was written all over her face—again. I wiped my hands on my jeans and shrugged. I knew my mother hated my paintings of Hades. I was glad to see my paintings up on the wall.

"Well, I paint more normal things than you think," I said, giving her my own look of annoyance. She walked into the orange and yellow kitchen and pointed to the one that I had painted during Winter break.

"I really liked this one though," she said, motioning to the one of Persephone and her mother. There was a wild garden with beautiful roses and daisies; things that I imagined with the spring and summer seasons. Persephone was looking back at the woods with a longing expression while Demeter, her mother, was leaning over the rose bush, plucking a blossomed rose. What my mother probably hadn't noticed was Hades, who was back in the forest. He was the one that Persephone was longing for.

"I haven't ever seen such a beautiful painting of the two," She announced, placing her hand on her chest. I heard her sharp intake of breath and softly released it, almost in a soft, relieving sigh; a sigh of pleasure and pride. She hadn't noticed Hades lurking in the background, and I kept my inner smile to myself, enjoying the hidden treasure in the picture. "You should paint things like this more."

I shrugged, mentally arguing with her that I have, but I knew to remain silent. My dad reminded me often to pick and choose my battles with my mom, and this was one I knew I'd lose. My room was littered with "those paintings;" My Hades paintings. I turned towards the door and out to the car to get another box full of my things from college.

"Just let it go for now. We'll get the rest of the boxes tomorrow. You have clean clothes laid out upstairs, and I put new sheets on your bed before I left to come get you."

I bit my lip, searching for the right words to allow me to escape to the ocean to paint. As happy as I was to be with her, I wanted my sanctuary – my escape. The one thing I dreamed of since the last time I had been home.

"Go on. I already know what you want to do," she said with a smile, eyeing the back door. "Just take a blanket with you, and don't be out too late." Before college, my mother would argue with me about going out at night to paint.

"You can't see! How can you paint in the dark?" I was always the one that argued back that I'd take a light, or sit under one of the spotlights on our dock. She hated me going out at night, and I didn't understand her fear.

"Someday, someone is going to kidnap you, and I won't even know that you're gone. I can't see you when you go out to the beach to paint. Can't you just wait until morning?"

Nighttime was the only time that I could think and feel. The paint wasn't just paint anymore. It was emotion and pain, fear and love. It was a smooth and creamy way of letting my soul escape and become a new form – a new person.

"I'll be fine," I'd say and roll my eyes at her. There was no one. It was always just me; me and the ocean and my canvas; my paints and my imagination.

"Are you sure you're okay with me going out tonight?" I asked, giving her a confused look. She nodded her head and gave me a smile.

"I'm sure. Just be back in by eleven."

I didn't hesitate or question her; I raced into my room for my watercolors that I stored under my bed, changed into one of my ripped up, smudged "St. Judith High School" shirts, shorts, and grabbed an empty canvas. I surveyed my room and noticed not much had changed since Spring Break. My mother made my bed, fixed my display pillows and stacked my white paper onto a small, neat pile on my painting desk. I noticed a few green paint swatches on my white coverlet, and I wondered if my mother freaked out when she saw that. I wondered how many times my mother tried to get rid of the stain and failed. There were a few new plants on my window sill; plants that I'm sure my mother dug up from the side garden and taken care of enough to get them to stay alive and put them in flower pots. My mother loved to litter our house with more than just relics of the Gods my family loved so much. She also loved flowers. She told me of her love for the feel of their petals, the feel of the green freshness they brought into the house.

"They're like extra children that I only have to water and watch grow," she once said to me. I smiled, remembering the sweet fragrance of ocean and flowers in the house during the summer, and anticipated it all the more.

I grabbed a few paintbrushes from the tiny, tin can on my desk and dashed from my door, down the steps, and out into the back yard, where our stone sidewalk led into the nothingness of sand and water. I hadn't bothered with shoes. The sand felt cool and rough against my feet, and I knew I was home. I couldn't stop the smile forming on my face as I tucked a strand of my hair behind my ear. The roar of the ocean was beautiful; a distant song that I missed. I set up my canvas and paint and closed my eyes, envisioning another scene from one of my father's stories. I pictured perfect Persephone, with her golden hair and blue eyes, looking at and into my dark God with a kind of love that was indescribable; it was a kind of love that I believed could heal broken hearts, could begin and end wars in ancient battlefields of old olive trees long forgotten now. I believed their love was the kind of love that could endure through time; the endless river of time and memories. I knew it was a painting that I would want in my room. I dipped my brush into the water that I collected in a water bottle from the ocean and began to wet the canvas with a fiery yellow, and a deep ocean blue.

It wasn't until I glanced up to look at the ocean, away from his face, that I saw a dark form standing near where the waves met the sand. I didn't know what made me look up from what I was doing, but now I was too nervous to look away. I flashed a glance back down at my painting, hoping that it was just a late-night walker or jogger who was admiring the beauty of the night. But when I glanced back up, the form was still standing there. For a moment, I thought that it was perhaps a washed up buoy or log, but the form stood silent and unwavering. The longer I stared at it, the more of a human shape it took on. The form was actually a person and just as I realized this, the person started to walk towards me, getting closer and closer. I began to see more clearly that it was a man.

The nervousness caught in my throat, and it was all I could do to swallow. My heart was pounding. I could hear my mother's voice echo in my ears. *'Someone could kidnap you, and I'd never know.'* I tried to picture the path behind me that led to the back door. I wondered how long it would take me to run to it.

"Hello?" I murmured, my voice shaking. The figure didn't reply. It stood silently, now closer to where I was sitting. "Can I help you with anything?" I carefully pushed my brushes into the water bottle and started to gather up my paints. The figure started to move closer, and I could feel my eyes begin to water. I was panicking. My breath was quickening, and all I could think to do was run or scream, but my body wasn't working. I couldn't move.

"Please, this isn't funny. What do you want?" I said with more urgency. The figure must have known or heard my fear, and it stopped. I could see an arm or a hand lift up, and I heard a faint, deep voice.

"I don't want to hurt you, Summer." I didn't want to know how the shape knew my name. I didn't bother to put my life on the line to ask the question. "You don't have to go." If the man honestly thought that I was going to bother to stay to see what he wanted now, he had to be crazy.

"I can see I must be bothering you. I'll just go inside now." I stated gently, testing my body and realizing I could finally move. I slowly stood up and tucked my painting underneath my arm.

"Please. Don't." The person whispered, and I noticed the figure was getting closer and closer to my light. If it came any closer, the figure would have a face. I could make out a faint detail in the silhouette, and could tell that it was a male's face. His nose was long and sharp, and his lips were a faint, deep line. His eyes stood out to me the most. They looked so familiar. They looked as if I had painted them a thousand times. They were a mix of blue and purple, and black. I knew that if I just looked down at my painting, I would see his face more clearly on my canvas than how he was before me. Could this truly be happening? The mere thought of all this scared me.

"Summer, please stay. I won't hurt you."

"Why should I stay? I don't know you."

He was silent and took one step closer toward the light. "But you *do* know me. You've known me for a long time." I watched him take another step.

"Please, stop," I commanded, backing up, feeling the sand mesh turn into the concrete under my feet. I knew that I was getting closer to the back door of my house. Safety was only a few feet away. "I think you have the wrong Summer." I could see the faint line of his lips turn into a small smile. This wasn't a joke.

"No, you're the Summer I've been looking for." He stepped into the light, and I was facing the spitting image of the same man that I had painted my whole life. He was dressed all in black with a matching cloak that billowed around him in the slight breeze from the ocean. His outfit made his pale skin stand out all the more. He looked like he had stepped out of some sort of vampire horror film. He looked dead. His lips were dark, and his hair was long, stringy, and fell onto his shoulders. It too was black.

"Do you recognize me now, Summer?" he whispered, catching my gaze.

I was holding my breath when I realized I couldn't find my voice. I felt the tears that had been on the brink of spilling from my eyes, trickle down my cheeks. I was dreaming. I *had* to be dreaming. This was the only way to explain it. I had to still be at school with Rachel, my roommate, sleeping soundly above me in our bunk beds. This could not really be happening.

"I think you do," he murmured, giving me a faint smile. My face must have said it all. "You're not dreaming. I'm real. You can touch me." He extended a pale hand out toward me, and I could only stare at it. His skin was creased with dark shadows. He was everything that spoke death, but I still felt the need to touch him. "Touch me, Summer," he whispered, walking closer to me.

I felt my hands let go of the water bottle and my painting, all clattering at my feet. I could feel the cool ocean water from the bottle spill over my toes. I could imagine the black water staining the white sand. I felt my hand stretch out to his, and my fingers touched his palm. His fingers wrapped around my wrist as my eyes met his the moment of impact.

"Are you really…" I couldn't even voice my own question completely. His eyes were telling me that I knew the truth. I already knew that if I glanced down at my painting, I'd see him. If I went into my room and looked at the paintings there, I'd see him. If I went into the kitchen and looked into the forest, I'd see his shadow. He was here, right in front of me.

"What do you want from me?" I asked, afraid of the answer.

"For you to come with me," he said.

I looked at him, confused. To go with him? Was this some jokester that my mother had hired to scare me? Was this her way of telling me that I had gone too far? I

19

wondered how much trouble she went through to make all of this happen. How had she found him? How much did she pay him? His voice interrupted my thoughts.

"Do you know the story?"

Story? I didn't want to think about it. I knew exactly what he was talking about. Instead, I wanted to close my eyes and wake back up at school or wake up in my room. It could be tomorrow. It could be anything but right now. I couldn't believe that this was really happening. As far as I was concerned, he couldn't be real. Not even if I had wished it as hard as I could. This couldn't really be happening.

"Story?" I whispered, closing my eyes. I could see the story play out in my mind as if I were there. I could see her, his wife; beautiful and blonde. Her eyes were open and curious. She was picking flowers with two of the most beautiful women in the land. Their wild curly hair, woven with crowns of flowers as they wore flowing silk dresses, caught in a gentle summer breeze as they gathered arrangements of flowers. There was one flower – one that stood out to Persephone the most, soft and red. She picked it and was engulfed in blackness, where the dark Lord lingered and waited. He was there: his face, his arms. He had her, and he was taking her down into his world, where he wanted me to go.

"You know the story, Summer," he acknowledged, almost as if he had just seen the images play out in my mind of what I always imagined. I could feel his other hand on my cheek, his fingers drawing on my skin. I did know the story. He had taken the maiden from earth into his underworld and made her his queen. He loved her. He wanted her. And then she was taken away from him. Her mother wanted her back. She ate seeds from a pomegranate; food that was in the underworld. Food of the dead, and that kept her connected with him always. She was to be shared for all eternity.

"What do you want with me?" I asked again, keeping my eyes closed. I didn't want to be hypnotized. I didn't want to feel anything more than the desire to run, but there was something that I couldn't explain keeping me there, within his grasp.

"You belong to me, Summer. You always have, even when you were taken away from me. Even then, you still belonged to me. This is how it's supposed to be. It was this way in the beginning, and it is how it will be in the end."

"I can't go with you," I said, pushing his hands off of me. I pushed myself away from him, and slowly backed toward my house. This was someone's awful joke. "If my mother hired you, you can tell her she wins." His face was confused for a moment and then he shook his head.

"Summer, no one hired me. Nothing that you know is what it seems. Trust me."

I shook my head, wanting to laugh at him. Trust him? Had he looked at himself in the mirror? He was the last person on earth that looked trustable.

"I'm not going to stand here and let you mock me," I snapped and turned toward the house, walking as fast as my feet could carry me. It wasn't fast enough. I wasn't fast enough. I felt his cold arms wrap around my waist, and his cool breath was on my neck. His touch was just as startling as the first time. He sent shivers down my spine.

"I won't let you go, Summer. You ate the seeds, and you belong to me. You have to fulfill the promise that was granted to me."

"I didn't eat any seeds. I don't know what you're talking about!" I shouted, trying to shove him off of me. "It's just a story!" I continued to try to get him off of me, but to no avail, he was much stronger than me.

"Our love isn't just a story, Summer. It's real. Don't you feel it?" I felt his hand press against my chest where my heart was, and it began to ache. I felt tears fill my eyes again, and I tried to struggle harder. "No! Stop it!"

"I've searched for you for years, Summer, and when I found you, I watched you. I watched you paint my face over and over again and knew that you had not forgotten about me. You know me, and deep down, you know the truth."

I fell to my knees, pressing my palms into my eyes. I was a mess of sand and water, and dried paint, and now of death. I felt his hands slip away, and I held my breath, counting to five. I needed to collect myself. "Wake up, Summer. Wake up." I whispered to myself, pressing my hands into my eyes again. I finally dropped my hands into the sand and opened my eyes. The only sound was the ocean and my heavy breathing. There was no voice. I was too afraid to turn around and see him standing there, but I knew I had to. I couldn't sit in the sand all night. I bit my lip and slowly turned my head to see nothing but the expanse of the night and the ocean. There was no one. My painting and paints were clattered together, next to the spilled water.

I crawled quickly to where my painting was, and collected my stuff. I stood up hastily, dusted the sand off of my knees and canvas and dashed into the house. The lights were off, and I knew my mother was in bed already. She hated staying up when my father was away. I locked the door and tested it twice before I quietly backed away, keeping the door in sight. I was so afraid I'd suddenly see his face like a scene in a horror film. I was afraid I'd hear his voice. *"You have to come with me."* I pressed the memory into the back of my head as I walked through the kitchen.

My painting on the wall stopped me from continuing to my room. Persephone's face wasn't just of longing anymore. It was of a fear that I now understood, and her mother's face wasn't of indifference. Her mother knew what was lurking. She was waiting to see what Persephone would choose. Would she choose love or death? I felt my breath hitch, and I knew what he said was true.

He was real, and he wanted me. I dashed up the stairs to my room and locked the door. Before I went to bed, I turned all my paintings around so I couldn't see his face, and make the encounter more real.

Chapter Three

"Aren't you going out to paint tonight?" my mother asked me gently as I picked at the TV dinner she made in the microwave. It was some sort of chicken potpie that looked more like puke with a crust. I lifted my gaze at her and shrugged.

"I think I'd rather stay in tonight. I'm kind of tired." That was a lie. I was very tired. I hadn't slept at all the night before. I was afraid to close my eyes and not wake in my bed. I was afraid I'd see his face when I slept though I knew even then, I would not escape him or his haunting shadow. In my dreams, he took my hand and led me into a dark cave with the echoing waters all around me. It was always the same cavern: vast and long; the waters formed a long river that seemed to go on and on into the darkness. Surprisingly, in these dreams, I always went willingly with him, and the willingness scared me. His pale face would meet my gaze and change into a dark warmth; a feeling of safety would wash over me, and I knew that I could trust him; I knew, even if only in dreams, I was safe there.

"You look it, honey. Maybe you need to stop staying up so late to paint."

I glanced up at her from the potpie and gave her a slight nod. I couldn't help but glimpse back down at the crusted dinner and pick at the glob of brown gravy and peas. I tried to hide my distress though I knew it was written all over my face. I wondered if I studied the pie long enough, my mom would confuse my distress for distaste in her choice of dinner options. Stirring the peas and carrots with my fork, all I could think was that Dad really needed to get home already.

"Your father really knows how to pick the TV dinners out, doesn't he?" my mother said with a faint laugh.

I gave her a slight smile with a nod. "Maybe we should make one for him when he gets home."

My mother nodded in agreement with me and laughed. I could already see her planning out the dinner for Wednesday night. "Maybe we should order some Chinese or something," She said as she stood up and dumped her paper plate full of mush into the trashcan. She came over and picked up my plate and did the same with mine.

"You can, Mom. I'm not really hungry," I murmured, pulling my hand through my brown hair. I was tired, and I didn't want to think about him anymore.

"I didn't get to see you at all today. You never came out of your room," my mother said, eyeing me as she pulled out the yellow phone book from the drawer next to the sink. I didn't know what to tell her. I couldn't tell her the truth that I had been too afraid to sleep, that was, until my body finally lost the battle and I drifted off. When I finally awoke, it had around been two in the afternoon. I spent a few minutes debating on whether I should get up and face the day or not. I finally forced myself to take a shower, and I supposed my mother was out in her gardens or at one of the farmer's markets, admiring someone else's flowers or fruits. I couldn't help but notice the few bananas and apples on the table, in one of the large bowls my mom usually had out during the summer months. On top of the bunch was a large pomegranate, plump and seasoned. It was unusual to see one of them during the summer months;

I studied it for a moment, wondering how my mother happened to come across one. When I had finally emerged from the long shower, I took a peek at myself, seeing the fear etched into my face. The fear was the dark circles under my brown eyes, and the few red spots, evidence of acne sprouting to life. I recognized the same expression Persephone had on her face in the painting in the kitchen. It was the same one I still wore.

"Sorry," I whispered, as I crossed my arms and lowered my head into them.

"Maybe you should just get some more sleep. I can order you something and leave it in the fridge. You can heat it up if you get hungry later tonight," she said with a smile and walked toward the phone. "Just go to bed, honey." She grabbed the phone and patted my back, pushing me out of my seat.

I walked out into the hallway, toward the staircase and gazed out the window as I started to climb the first step. The ocean was at high tide and was close to our house. The rolling waves in and across the shore were still so beautiful to me. It was as beautiful as the countless nights I would spend with my dad on the beach. He would take me out in the moonlight, and we'd collect as many seashells as we could. In the early morning hours, sometimes he would awaken me, and we'd try to watch little sea turtle babies make their journey into the ocean. I wrapped my arms around myself and sighed, suddenly missing my father terribly. I could almost smell the salt in the air, and at least, that was comforting. I always wanted to have that smell in the house I lived in. It was tempting to turn around and go out to the ocean to paint, but the fear of knowing that there was more than just the ocean outside of our house stopped me. My eyes scanned the large expanse of the beach, looking for only one thing, or rather--person. My eyes stopped looking when they fell onto a large shadow. It could have been anything, but my mind instantly saw his face. I felt my heart start to beat faster, and I leaned closer to the window. Was that him? Was he standing there watching me? I squinted with the attempt of trying to see what it was.

"Honey? What are you looking at?" My mother's voice startled me, and I jumped back. She was standing in the hallway with the phone on her chest with a confused look written on her facial features. I took a quick glance back out the window for a moment and saw the shadowy figure was gone, almost as if on cue.

"Summer?" She said more sternly, and I turned back toward her.

"Nothing," I began, trying to sound believable. "I was just looking at the ocean."

"So intently?" She questioned concern wrinkling in the corners of her eyes. There was a disbelief written on her face, and I knew she didn't believe me. She walked toward me with the obvious intent that she was heading for the window to have a look for herself. "Are there kids running around out there again?" I shook my head, watching as she leaned in toward the window to have a look. "There were a few kids a couple weeks ago that were pretty rowdy out there. Your dad went out and gave them a good scare."

I wanted to say that it was probably nothing like the scare that I had last night but decided against it. I didn't want her to know to anything. Who would believe me anyway? "No, Mom. No one is out there. I promise. Just the ocean," my voice spoke automatically, wanting the conversation to be over. I shouldn't have given the ocean a second glance. I knew I should have gone straight to my room, and perhaps then she'd be watching *Home and Gardens* on the television, and I could be starting a new painting, or even just resting. The Gods knew that I was exhausted.

She put her hand on my shoulder and nudged me toward the stairs. She probably thought I was seeing things because of my lack of sleep. I wanted her to be right. I wanted to just blame it all on the lack of sleep. I hadn't really had a good night's sleep in a long time; last night included. All the projects, all the painting, school, papers, and now being back home. It was a lot all at once. I didn't make her tell me to go to bed again. I climbed the steps. As I walked toward my door, I turned back to see my mother glancing out of the window again. I wondered what she was looking at. Did she see it too?

"Mom?" I asked, and watched as she turned toward me with a look of concern. "Is everything okay?"

She gave me a nod and a small smile. "I'll see you in the morning."

I nodded, and silently went into my bedroom, closing the door behind me. I waited until I heard her footsteps head back toward the kitchen to move. I knew she was fully distracted when I heard the hum of her voice on the phone. I pushed the extra sheets of white paper out of the way on my desk, as I pulled the first one from on top of the pile and gently spread it out in front of me. I pulled a large, black paintbrush and dipped it into my day-old water. I usually always had water in a cup by my desk, just in case, I suddenly had the urge to paint.

The smell of the oil paint filled my room, and it felt familiar and comforting. I could forget about everything that happened until I started to paint him. It was as if my hands were working against me. They wanted to show me him again and again. Each new sheet of paper painted the image of his face: His eyes, his stringy hair, his lips, and his nose. He was everywhere. I could feel myself start to panic again. I grabbed another sheet, trying to draw anything else, but my hand was already drawing the same, familiar face. He was there on my paper, more alive, more real than before. I could hear his voice whispering into my ear, *"You belong to me, Summer."* I closed my eyes, trying to block the voice.

I threw the paintbrush, and spilled the water, feeling a few drops fall onto my lap while the rest dribbled across my desk and down onto the floor. I tried to block the memory of his hands, his arms, and his touch, and I had been so close to winning until I heard a faint rustle coming from the other side of my room. I held my breath and slowly turned toward the sound. When I opened my eyes, his eyes were staring into mine.

"You never came," he declared softly, as his arms trapped me to the desk. "I waited for you. I saw you, yet you didn't come out to me."

I glared at him. I didn't like that he was so close to me. "I won't come with you. I won't ever come back out again!"

He smiled at me and shook his head. "Summer, when will you ever learn? These matters are far beyond your control. There is no point in avoiding me. I will always come to you. I know where you are, and I know where you will be."

"If that's true, then why are you showing up now? If my fate is to be with you, why now?" I felt his hand graze my cheek for a moment.

"I had to wait for you to be the right age."

I slowly stood up from my chair, forcing him to back away. I grabbed the desk behind me. He followed, his gaze never leaving mine.

"The right age? Are you serious? And you think nineteen is acceptable?"

He didn't say anything. He sighed and walked to my window beside my bed. His silence was eerie and uncomfortable.

"You're nuts; you know that?" I said, looking around my desk while his back was turned for any sort of weapon I could use if I needed to. "I don't even know who you are. How did you even get in here?"

He exhaled again but didn't turn back around to face me. "You know who I am. Why are you so against acknowledging the fact that I might just actually be real?" he asked. I could feel him raising his eyebrow at me. I could see his faint reflection in the window. His eyes were full of a sadness that was old and deep. They looked regretful and angry; a very powerful combination.

"You never said who you were," I pushed. I needed to hear him say who he was, to clarify I wasn't crazy. I needed to know I hadn't imagined any of this. I needed to know he was real.

"I am Hades or Pluto. Whichever name you prefer," he said nonchalantly. His indifference stunned me, and I sat back down in my chair, watching him stand so coolly in front of my window.

"What did you say?" I asked in disbelief. This guy really had to be crazy to be saying things like that. I wanted to put as much distance between him and me as I could. He seemed to relish in my discomfort.

"You heard what I said," he said with a smug smirk.

"How did you get in here?" I asked again, watching as he turned around slowly and shrugged, lifting his hands.

"You wouldn't believe me even if I told you the truth, now would you?"

I scanned his dark appearance again. He looked warmer than he had the night before. His lips weren't so dark; they had a hint of pink warmth. His eyes weren't so black; they speckled green and gold in the blackness of his irises.

"You just came into my bedroom, thinking that it would be okay?" I tried to find my voice, to control my shock but it seemed useless, even more so as I watched his facial expression change into amusement. He must have known that I would be angry. His lips turned in a slight smile. This angered me more.

"I could just as easily scream for my mother who is just downstairs." I tried to sound threatening, but I was quickly shot down. He shook his head and crossed his arms.

"And I could just disappear, and she'd say that you were dreaming." He taunted.

"Good, if it means you'll disappear, then I'll scream," I said, standing up and walking toward the door. I wanted my scream to echo throughout the large house. No matter where she was, she'd hear me. He followed me and stopped me, wrapping his arms around my waist and bringing my body closer against his. His long hand was suddenly around my mouth. I could faintly smell the salt on his skin from the ocean. His touch wasn't as cold as it had been the night before but still had the same powerful impact. His chest felt hard, and I knew that I wouldn't win the fight if I tried to struggle again.

"Please do not," he began. "You already know that if you do scream, and I disappear, I'll always come back again. I'll keep coming back until you agree to go with me." His eyes spoke the truth.

"I hate to burst your bubble, but I won't ever agree to go with you," I said as I pushed his hand away from my mouth. He didn't let go of my hand. Instead, he interlaced his fingers with mine. It felt odd and wrong, and I dug my fingernails into his hand, hoping he'd let go. He smiled and held onto my hand tighter.

"Then I'll just have to take you," he promised slowly, with a smirk on his pink lips.

"And then have the police come after you? You're making some great life-changing decisions for yourself."

He gave me a curt smile. "They won't find me. They won't even know where to look. No mortal does."

"For being a professional actor, you really don't know when it's time to stop the act, do you?"

"I'm not acting," he snapped. I knew I had angered him more. I could feel his body tighten; his hand held onto mine harder. "When are you going to believe it, Summer? What do I have to do to prove to you that I am him," he pointed to the paintings littering my walls. "I am the man that you paint – the man that you love."

"I don't love you," I whispered harshly. His face fell, and I instantly felt bad. His touch became gentle, and his hand slipped away from mine. His sad eyes drifted over my face; I could feel the hair on my neck stand up.

"You're so beautiful. Just as beautiful as you were before." I looked at him confused. *Before?* "I was wrong to expect that you would love me, the way that I love you."

"But you don't know me," I whispered, my voice trembling. He searched my eyes, bringing his hand to my cheek and gently caressing it. I hated his touch. I wanted him to stop.

"Yes, I do know you. I know you better than anyone else does." I wanted to test him. I wanted to hear the answers only I would know. Not even my mother or student peers from school would be smart enough to guess. I wanted to know what he knew.

"You know me better than anyone else? How could you?" I pushed his hand away from my face, and I felt his hands let me go. I escaped to the confines of my bed, and I watched as he sat in my chair next to my desk. Distance was good.

"I've known you your whole life, and even before then," he said, watching me.

"What do you know?" I stammered. He leaned toward the paintings against my wall and started to go through each. I felt my cheeks turn hot. Each painting was of him. Each had a secret that I only knew. When he reached the last one, he pulled it out and faced it toward me. It was a painting of a brown haired girl, standing beside a tall man, dressed in black.

"You knew I'd come all along, didn't you, Summer? You hoped I'd come for you." The painting was only evidence to his argument. How could I dismiss it? How could I deny what was right in front of me?

"You never answered the question," I stated slowly, waiting. I held my breath as he moved across the room toward me, and sat down beside me on my white coverlet.

"I know each and every painting that you've made. Even the ones your mother hasn't seen."

"How—" He interrupted me, lifting his finger gently back to my lips. I stopped, waiting for him to continue. I saw him eyeing my lips, and I wondered what he was thinking.

"I could tell you all the things that I'm sure your friends could say if they were asked this question. Things like your favorite color, food, things like that. A number of times you've been to Greece. A number of times you've seen your favorite movie. But I feel like all of those things wouldn't matter to you, because that's basic knowledge, and if I'm a God, I'm supposed to know all the little details that everyone overlooks." He was right, so I waited.

"You can only sleep on your side," he whispered. "I've watched you struggle to sleep, and every time you lay on your side, you instantly fall under the spell." His finger traveled to my hair, and he gently wrapped a few strands around it. I wanted to push him away. I hated his touch. I hated how he felt that he could touch me so easily as if he could do whatever he wanted to me, and I wouldn't say

34

anything. He looked as if he knew my unease, and yet continued to enjoy being near me.

"You and your mother don't get along at all. You tolerate her. When you left for college, it was all you could think of. She didn't understand your love for me, and Summer, she never will. I'm the dark thing in life. Death. The darkness that is to be feared by humans. But I'm much more than just death to her. You won't understand right now, but someday you will." My eyes were wide. No one knew my real feelings toward my mother. I hadn't ever voiced them, not even to myself.

"What else can you tell me?" I whispered, wanting to test more of his knowledge.

"I haven't proven myself to you yet?" he asked with a look of amusement on his face.

"Why me?" I asked. It was the question I asked over and over again in my mind all day. Why me? What had made me so desirable to him? What was it about me that he wanted so badly? I had made my whole life about him. I had spent hours painting him, loving him, pretending to have conversations with him. He must have known about it all if he truly was Hades. He eyed me for a moment. I could tell he was searching for the right words.

"There is more to this world than you think, little one," he whispered. His gaze drifted to my hair that he was playing with. I lifted my hand to his, the first touch from me. He didn't move at my touch. He was lost in a world that I didn't understand, or couldn't see. I felt the strange desire to hold him.

"Can't you explain?" I asked as I fought the urge. I kept my hand on his. He shook his head; his silence was unnerving.

"I won't keep the secrets from you, but you have to be the one to discover them."

"What secrets?"

"And this is why you must come with me," he said, pulling away from me. He fell back on the bed beside me and closed his eyes. "I'll give you some time to think about it, but after a month has gone by, you'll have no choice."

"So, you're basically giving me a month to go willingly with you?" I asked, looking down at his still form. He nodded gently.

"Yes. One month."

I sat there, thinking about what one month meant to me. One month of freedom. One month of the ocean, my father's laughter. One month of junk food and oil paints. One month was a very short time.

"What about my parents? My school?" I asked, eyeing my wall full of my paintings. In one month, they would be the only thing left of me.

"I suppose you would worry about those things," he began, gazing at me and then away, rubbing his chin with his forefinger and thumb. "Those things are unimportant, as you will come to find, where I shall be taking you." I wanted to argue, and he seemed to understand my facial expression.

"Can't you see, Summer? There is always a larger plan, a better plan compared to the one that you humans chart for yourselves. You'll just have to trust me. The way humans were always supposed to." He must have wanted some sort

of reaction from me given the way his body language spoke
to me. He wanted to be feared, or remain unquestioned. It
was only in my nature to do the opposite of what he
wanted. I wasn't one of his "followers" who were willing to
do exactly as he said, or exactly as only God or Goddess
would command. There were too many stories enriched
with the clear message to think for oneself, and not listen to
any of the Greek Gods. I was quiet even as he murmured,
"In all the time I have *been*, I have found very few things
that are worthy of such a sacrifice, but I feel like this is one
of those things." I sighed, feeling a shiver crawl down my
spine. A bad feeling turned my stomach into knots; it was a
feeling of dread that I could not explain.

"You should probably sleep," he said, patting the
pillow beside him.

"Are you leaving?"

"Do you want me to leave?" he asked with a gentle
look of concern. "Does my presence bother you?"

"Do you want the truth or the lie?" I asked as I pulled
the pillow away from him and stood up, pushing the
coverlet back and crawling back into the warm spot that my
body had created from sitting there for so long.

"Whichever you feel like telling me," he murmured,
sliding away from me to give me the distance that I secretly
wanted. I pulled my pillow in front of me, making it my
newest defense shield from him.

"Just as long as you're not here in the morning," I
yawned. I heard him chuckle faintly.

"I can see what I can do."

I turned onto my side, and just as he had predicted, I
was asleep in moments.

Chapter Four

There was a pounding on my door that startled me from sleep. The sun was bright and was blinding me from seeing anything. My first thought was the pounding. What did my mother want? She usually never woke me up. I pushed myself up onto my elbows and glanced around the room. My alarm clock beside my bed read 9:42 a.m.

"Summer, are you awake?" I heard my mother call through my bedroom door. I pushed the covers out of the way, releasing myself from the cocoon I made for myself during the night. The instant I sat up, I remembered the night before; the man appearing in my room. His presence when I fell asleep. I turned toward the window and saw nothing. There was no trace of him anywhere. My nightstand was clear, the window closed. Nothing was out of place. It was as if he never had been there to begin with. The thought sent a shiver racing down my spine. How easily could he blend into the world without ever being noticed?

"Summer?" I heard my door crack open, and my mother's hopeful eyes met mine. "Oh, good. You are awake," she said with a tart smile. I could only give her a sleepy nod.

"What's the matter?" I asked, letting out a small yawn. My mother's smile grew wider.

"Your father just called." He was calling pretty early. My mind quickly calculated the time difference. It was 3:42 in the afternoon there. I guess it made sense.

"Is everything alright?" I asked, half expecting to hear he had found a new artifact and would be bringing it back

38

over to the United States early. That meant real dinners. It was very normal for him to come home early from trips, and I enjoyed getting news like that. My mother nodded as she came and sat down on my bed next to me.

"Your dad was offered a new job!" She looked like she was high on life as she let the words escape her lips. Her expression was so full of excitement that I supposed she was ready to run a marathon out of the pure joy she was feeling. She looked like she was ready to run a marathon. Usually, my mother was more jealous of my dad for his new cases that kept him in Greece. It made her remember her days of studying and traveling with him. They were a team. They were always together until she had me. I came along and changed the two-pack-team into a trio. I always felt that my mother resented me for changing the family dynamics in this way. I was the child that she had to stay at home for. I was the child that held her back from being in Greece with my father. There were times that my mother would mention that she had to stay in the United States for me; her face would grow distant and cold, and a jolt of guilt would run through me. I would push my bangs out of my face, and try to tell myself that I wasn't a mistake, even if my mother made me feel like I was the error that ruined her life with my father.

"That's great Mom," I said with a smile. "What's he going to be doing?"

"We're moving to Greece," she blurted out, avoiding my question. "We're going to go stay with him. Isn't that great? That means I can go out to the sites with him again!"

Greece. *Greece.* Great as a vacation spot. Great for people like my parents; they could dig until their hearts

39

were content, but for a college student like me? Live in Greece? I couldn't picture myself among the rubble and ruins with them, and I couldn't bear the thought of painting all that rubble and ruin either. I knew my only solace in Greece would be the oceans, and I suddenly prayed that wherever we lived, I'd be near a large body of water. The water would be my escape away from my mother and her insistence of rummaging around in the dirt to find artifacts with my dad. "What about school?" I said quietly. My mother's smile grew wider. She was beginning to look like the Grinch as he devised a new plan to steal Christmas. My mother was about to steal my life.

"You could study art there! Think how exciting that would be. You could study the classics!"

"I've already studied the classics—"

"Europe invented art!" She interrupted, thinking she was making a point. She didn't know anything about the origins of art.

"No, Europe did not invent art, mother," I whispered, sliding my hands through my hair and over my face. I wanted to push her out of my room and go back to sleep. This also had to be a dream. I was living one long nightmare that I couldn't wake up from.

"Summer!" she whined, slapping her thighs with her hands. She was upset that I wasn't excited as her. "It's only for a year!"

"I don't want to drop out of school," I said with determination. "You can't just expect me to be jumping for joy." It wasn't as if I had any choice about leaving school at this point anyway. I was still trying to determine if the man who had claimed to be Hades was truly real, or if I had dreamed all of the encounters. Everything was happening so fast, and both of the occurrences happened in a haze of darkness. If he were real, I'd have to leave everything behind here. There was no escaping change, whether it was created by him or by my family. But I wanted to try to stand my ground.

"Honey, I promise we will find you a great art school to go to." There was an assurance in her voice, but I didn't know if I should really believe her. She didn't know anything about art school, and what made a good art school. It was much more than just painting and drawing well. It meant being surrounded by people who had the same goals; wanted the same things.

"When does he want us to move there?" I asked, slowly pushing my bed hair away from my face. I hated feeling like I was giving into her, but what choice did I have? I knew she had to win in the end. I would save my dad a long distance telephone call, in which I knew he would insist that I apologize to her for my behavior, and I'd have to happily agree to all of her terms. Her face lit up and grasped my hands; the same way a woman from a Jane Austen movie would have. It was as if I had just told her, *'Yes Mom, I'll go with you!'* without actually saying those words.

"He asked us to start cleaning up the house. Close it up, pack, ship and fly as soon as we could."

"We're keeping the house?" I asked in disbelief. "Can we afford to live in a house in Greece and keep our house?"

She gave me a smile. "You let me and your father worry about that," she said as she patted my knee. I felt like I was on a joke of an episode of *Full House* for a moment.

41

My mother never did things like that. She never displayed her affection for me. I watched her with wary eyes as she stood up, letting out a sigh of relief.

"Well, I guess we better start packing things up."

"Are we coming back?" I asked, not wanting to give in. I didn't want to show that I was agreeing to anything yet, but I knew by the look on my mother's face that I was beyond reasoning with her. She was determined to make this move. I watched her as she started walking toward my door. She turned at the door and shrugged.

"I'm not sure. It's not like we have anything here anyway," she said, extending her hands out toward the room. She was right. All of our family lived far away, and none had talked to us in years. My father's side wasn't a fan of my mother. They saw my mother as a bad influence on my father. His family had wanted him to be a doctor or be someone of worth to make his family appear look well educated and successful. I always assumed it had something to do with status and how much influence he would have on others. My mother told him to follow his dreams, and he did. They never talked to them after they were married. My mother lost her parents a few years ago in a fire, leaving me grandparent-less. I didn't mind not having a grandmother to bake cookies with, or whatever you did with them. I didn't know what I was missing, though, I did hate the "Grandparents Lunch" that our school sometimes held. There would be a line of old, grey-haired men and women gathering to see their grandchildren, and I'd be one of the few students who didn't have a grandparent to sit with.

"You should try to decide what paintings you're taking if any at all. You could always make new ones and decorate your new room differently," she murmured, glancing around my room at the dark depictions of *his* face. "Have you painted anything new?" I watched her inch toward my painting desk and lean over to look at the sheets of white paper. "I like this one." She patted the first sheet of paper on the stack.

I remembered my sudden dash of tried paintings the night before; all of which had taken shape into his face until he appeared in my room out of thin air. It occurred to me then that nothing was finished in the stack, and for the few pieces that were, they were all paintings of the subject she didn't like. What could possibly be there for her to enjoy?

"Which one?" I asked confused. She lifted the sheet up to expose a very beautiful woman.

"Is this a self-portrait?" My eyes gazed at the painting I hadn't drawn. The woman was standing under a tall tree, with beautiful red, round fruit hanging from the branches. She had soft brown hair that seemed to be blowing in the invisible wind. Her eyes were dark and warm, and very familiar. She was dressed in the kinds of clothing I saw in my Greek History books: long, flowing white robes with golden ropes and extravagant jewelry that glittered in her hair and on her neck.

"I was…" My voice drifted into a mumble of nothing and my mother smiled.

"Can I take this and hang it up?"

I stood up, closing in on the distance between her and me. I wanted to grab it out of her hands before it

43

disappeared from my room. It was mine. "No!" I said, reaching out for the painting. "It's not done. Plus, you can't hang it up. We're moving, remember?"

"I could hang it up in our new house."

"I don't want it hung up. It's not done," I persisted.

My mother pursed her lips and lowered the painting back down onto the table gently. She turned and left my room without a word. She hated when I refused her my artwork. If only she knew this wasn't mine. I peeked over the desk, glancing at the painting of the woman again. She was beautiful. I felt like I was looking at a woman who was only a reflection of me; a person that was asleep.

I glanced over my desk, checking my brushes and paints. Everything was where I left them before. I lifted the picture, exposing my half-drawn paintings. They were all of him. I wondered what he thought when he saw them. I wondered if this was how he saw me. Or Persephone? I lowered his painting back down onto my desk, taking a last quick look at it one more time.

Chapter Five

I rolled the last of my shirts into my suitcase. I had enough clothes to get me through two weeks. I was hoping we'd get our boxes by the time I ran out of my clean clothes, and we probably would, as long as my mother mailed them to our new home in Greece in time. Some of my paintings were lined up in a small box on my floor, next to my bed. His painting was first in line. Ever since my mother told me about my father's new job, Hades had not appeared to me. There was nothing but the still quietness of the night and the ocean waves for two weeks. I went to the ocean often and silently waited in the shadows for the one long, dark figure to appear, but he never came. Not even a breath on my neck as I curled into my covers before I fell asleep. I don't know why I waited or wanted him to appear, but it was a desire that I couldn't resist. It was just like waiting for a boy that you admired to call.

Today would be my last day in Judith Point – my last day on my beach. Tonight would be my last night sleeping in my own bed. It was a day of a lot of 'lasts.'

My mother tapped on my door, and as I turned to look at her, she greeted me with a warm smile. She seemed a lot happier since the news. She had lists of things she wanted to do as soon as she got Greece, and lots of things to eat; Greek salad with tons of feta cheese and olives were on the top of her list. My stomach churned at the thought of feta cheese and olives. I liked my American burgers and pizza, and I knew I would truly miss them. There was nothing like familiar comfort food.

"Got everything packed?"

"Mostly everything," I said, closing the last of my suitcases on the bed.

"Are you packing all of those?" She pointed to my box of paintings and bent over, scanning through the canvases. I already knew that when she looked up at me, her face would be full of disappointment. Most of them were of *him*. Except for the one that he made for me.

"I guess your pallet hasn't changed much," she said, standing up and giving me the look I predicted. Her eyes scanned my walls; with the paintings I was willing to leave behind; the more normal ones that she liked.

"I'm glad to see you're packing your self-portrait. We could hang that up in our new house."

"I think I'd rather keep it in my room."

She bit her lip at my reply. "Is there anything else that you'd like me to take to the post office today? This is probably the last run I'm going to make since we leave tomorrow."

I just looked down at my box at my feet and shrugged. "Just that one, everything else is clothes that are coming with me tomorrow." My mother looked satisfied. She bent back over, picking up the box and balancing it on one leg as she looked at me.

"What about your paints? Are they packed in a box or are you taking them with you as a carry-on or something?"

I tapped one of my suitcases. It seemed a little pathetic I had to have a suitcase completely full of my paints, and I felt almost ashamed of myself, but I knew I wanted them safe and sound, and I was not about to leave my only passion and comfort back on the shores of another country. I didn't want to have to wait a week to get my paints. I wanted them instantly. She rolled her eyes as if she expected me to pull something like that.

"Dinner will be a little late. I have to run these over, and then I need to run over to the travel agency and pick up our information there," she said as she glanced at her watch, turning to go out the door.

"Or we can do a 'get-your-own' night." She murmured as she left. "Either way, I'll be out."

At least, it was only going to be one more night of her fast food. Then we'd be back with my dad who could cook and held family dinners. I missed those a lot. I sat down on the edge of my bed and glanced around the almost empty space. Strangely, I wanted nothing more than to suddenly hear his voice in the corner of my room, and have someone to talk to about all of this. Moving to Greece was a big step for me. It meant giving up my school, my education, and it meant learning how to live in a different country. I pushed my fingers through my hair and held back the tears that were forming in my eyes. I heard my mother close the front door, and a few minutes later, the car started and pulled out of our gravel driveway.

The house was silent. *Too silent.* I imagined that it was already tomorrow. The house would be alone and quiet just like this. I felt a twist of anger and resentment tightening in my stomach. I was angry that I had to leave everything behind and sad; sad to be leaving my childhood home behind. It was all I could do to hold back the tears from surfacing. My mind and soul were as deep as the sea outside my window, and would flood over at any moment. I was feeling too many things and had no solid way of expressing them any longer. When I painted, all I painted was Hades. When I slept, all I dreamt of was the sea and the future green land awaiting me in a day. I felt another wave of anger fill my chest, and all I could think about was how selfish my parents were being. Why couldn't I just go back to school? I could stay here for the summer and be perfectly fine. I could easily find a job in town at the fish deli or the small grocery store, and I could pay bills. I knew that my parents would want to sell the house eventually, and perhaps they could just sell it to me. It couldn't be that hard to buy a house, let alone a house from my parents. And when it was time to go back to school, I could drive myself up and just stay there. They could go to Greece and dig and search for rocks and statues while I stayed behind at my ocean and painted. It seemed all logical to me. It seemed every time I brought the idea up to my mother; she thought I'd burn the house down.

"What if something happened, Summer? Who would you call?"

"The police or the fire department, I guess. If it wasn't something so urgent, I could call the neighbors. It wouldn't be as if I'd be all alone."

"No. Your father planned out a room just for you, and a place for you to paint. It'll be great. Just trust me."

I pressed my palms against my eyes and let out a deep sigh. I just had to trust everything would work out. Everything would fall into place, and I'd still be able to go to school and finish what I started at art school. My mother reminded me that this could be a chance for me to finally make friends. It could be a new start to my life. The only thing she didn't know was that I had made a friend; a strange friend, but none-the-less, a friend. Was I really calling him my friend? He was probably much less than a friend, and more of a stalker. He was also someone that I felt connected to – someone that I wanted to see again before I left for Greece. Did he know my family's plan? I felt a shiver run down my spine, and it felt like a finger was tracing my neck.

I stood up, glancing at my bed where I'd been sitting. I was expecting to suddenly see him; his long hair that touched his shoulders, and his pale skin that was cold. It almost reminded me of when skin was submerged in water for too long. The pale yet soft quality skin developed the longer it remained under the waters. He was as flawless as a reflection seen in the clearest waters, and yet, there was something about him that caused him to be blemished. It was beyond his eyes or features but in his soul. It was hidden in the darkest part of his eyes, in the crook of the corner of his lips; a secret that he seemed to want me to guess – to know.

I opened the small suitcase full of my paint supplies and pulled out a few colors and a few brushes, along with a white sheet of paper that was lying on my now empty desk. Painting always made me feel better, and I hoped this last time, it would have the same effect on me. This would be the last painting on my beach. I decided that I wanted to get comfortable, and out of my dusty clothes from cleaning and packing. I put my paints on my desk and walked to my dresser in the corner of my room. I pulled out clothes that I was willing to leave behind; a pair of sweats that were cut at the knees, and an extra-large shirt that had droplets of black and blue paint all over it. I pulled my hair up in a ponytail, and slipped on a pair of my old sneakers that also weren't being packed. I looked like a painter. The same way Maggie had displayed 'painter' with her overalls. I gave a small smile at the thought of her; I wondered what she was doing now that she was home. I could imagine Maggie with some of her friends from home; the faceless girls created in my mind, as they dove into crystal clear pools. Beach parties were planned, while eating pizza and watching the sunsets. I also knew Maggie would be there with her camera, capturing pictures for later to paint. Even though Maggie and I weren't the closest of friends, I knew I'd miss her. A piece of something familiar I'd never have again.

I grabbed my pile of paints, brushes and paper, and went down the stairs to the kitchen. It was dimly lit by the sun streaming in from the windows. There were hardly any decorations on the walls anymore, and only my mom's good dishes were in the open cabinet. She figured plastic plates were the best to pack and shipped them right away, while the china would be boxed carefully later and sent in more secure circumstances. A cruel part of me hoped a plate would get chipped on the way to Greece. My painting of Demeter and Persephone was still on the wall. I had insisted to leaving it behind. It still sent chills throughout my body. It was more a reminder of what *he* promised than any other painting I created. I stood there for a moment, looking at my brush strokes of the two women and the blurred shadow in the forest. The same shadow I wanted to see. I closed my eyes, taking in a deep breath of air. The ocean breeze coming from the open kitchen window filled my lungs. I was going to miss this place so much.

I opened my eyes, and slowly moved away from the painting. I wanted to escape to my ocean and spend as much time as I could. When I opened the back door to our porch, I saw that it was covered with a light dusting of sand. I pressed my toes into the rough grains, enjoying the feeling against my skin. There was something about sand and the beach that brought calmness to me.

I was glad when the walkway finally became sand and beach, and there was nothing solid underneath my feet. There was nothing ahead but the water and me. I set my collection of art supplies on the dry cement and pushed myself out toward the water. I loved the feeling of the ocean ebb over my feet. It brought back memories of my childhood. My father would take me out back to our ocean and build me sand temples instead of castles, and mermaid tails. He'd tell me the stories about the Gods who littered our house as we'd bury our feet in the moist sand. There were many times that my father would have to hold onto me just so that I wouldn't be washed away with the water. My mother would stand at the back door and watch. She was always watching, and he always played with me. He was my entertainer, and my mother was my keeper. I could see the picture of my father and me when I was seven. He had me on his shoulders and my feet were dripping with sand. I had since lost the photo, but had always wanted to paint my version of it. It was my favorite memory of the two of us.

I heard a seagull cry out over the roar of the waves, and the wind tasted sweet and salty as I took in a deep breath. This is how I always wanted to remember my beach; warm and peaceful, perfect: mine. I couldn't bring myself to turn around and grab my paints. I wanted to enjoy the beauty of it all without having to worry that I mixed the colors right, or added too much water on my brush. This sight was meant only for me. The world had created a painting for me to enjoy. I found a dry spot of sand and sat down, digging two holes with my toes for my feet to rest in. The more I dug, the more I thought, and the more I thought, the angrier I became. I had lived here my entire life. Even when I went away to Art School, I still had the promise of home waiting for me only an hour away. Home would be in Greece now.

Anger pushed me from the ground. Anger pushed me to grab my paints from the porch and scorch my paper with flashes of reds and yellows and angry orange. The dark purples felt like bruises that would never leave my body. They would be engrained into my skin, even the purple paint smeared on my thumb. Anger pushed me to cover the white paper until there was nothing but a mess of paint and water. Anger pushed me to tear apart the paper and dash it over the ocean foam. The pleasure and pain emerged as the waves tore and disintegrated the paper into nothing.

I felt my stomach twist and grumble, and I knew I was hungry. With a soft sigh, I turned around; taking only one more glance at the deep blue waves and wished for a moment that I had been born a fish. The ocean could have been my home. I wouldn't ever have to say goodbye to it. With that thought, I walked back toward the porch, watching my feet kick the sand with each step. I knew I'd have to ride my bike into town if I wanted to get something to eat or I could hope that there was something in the fridge. Maybe she had left something in there, thinking of me. It was cooler in the house than before I had gone out to the ocean. My feet were leaving a trail of sand on the kitchen floor, and I knew that if I didn't clean it up, my mother would have a fit.

I grabbed one of the dishrags lying by the sink. Getting it wet, I tried to wipe away as much sand as I could. I bent over, wiping away the sand on the bottoms of my feet. I tossed the rag on the counter and walked toward the fridge, expecting to find it completely empty. The fridge's air felt good against my warm skin as I glanced around the empty shelves. There was only a large lonely, pomegranate on the top shelf. It was a deep, blood red, and it made my mouth water. I was so leery of the tempting fruit. I knew the stories, and I knew what it symbolized. My hand reached for it, almost as if it acted despite my mind's protests.

My fingers squeezed the fruit and felt the firmness. I felt as if my body was acting without permission. My hands pulled open the silverware drawer and pulled out one of our dull knives that my mother was leaving behind. I set it on a dull orange plate from our cupboard and slowly cut into the fruit. It leaked red and looked as if the fruit was bleeding. A tiny seed popped from the wound I had made, and I gently picked up the seed, eyeing it. So much had revolved around such a small object. I resisted the strange desire to try a seed, and I began to cut into the fruit more. I stabbed the knife into it deeper, causing the fruit to break apart and expose a group of tiny red seeds. I pulled the white membrane away from the red seeds and started to collect them in a tiny bowl.

Each seed looked fresh, and I could almost taste the sweetness on my tongue. I stared at the little pieces of fruit until I finally found myself again, and threw them away in the trash bin. I grabbed the plate and tossed the rest of the pomegranate. I knew I needed to focus on what tomorrow would bring: an end to one life and a start to another. Hades and his seeds would have to be what I would face tomorrow.

Chapter Six

"Are you all set? Do you have yourself buckled in?"
My mother's voice startled me as I dashed my face away
from the airplane window. She asked me the question if I
was set over and over again before we left the house. At
that time, I glanced around the empty room, trying to find a
reason to stay. A reason to buy more time; but I found
none. I walked to my window, looking out over the dark
ocean, and clicking the window lock into place. Had it only
been two weeks since he'd come to see me? Was that just a
dream?

I felt my mother's hand on mine, and it brought me
back to her. The lack of sleep was apparent on my face. I
had neglected all forms of makeup, and my hair was pulled
up in a slight, messy ponytail. I felt tired and worn down,
and I knew I looked the part. It could have been the jet lag,
or perhaps just that packing had taken a lot out of me.
Thankfully the trip was almost over. We started in the
airport bright and early, departing on our first plane at 9:50
in the morning, and we were supposed to be landing in
Athens, Greece at 2:00 in the afternoon. When we changed
planes in London, I changed my watch to their time to be a
bit closer to the time we'd be living in. I knew that as the
plane flew over the countless towns and lights, minutes that
I could have slept were lost. We were landing, that I knew,
and that was good enough. The airplane started to shake a
bit more than normal, and it felt like we were taking a
quick nosedive right towards the ground below. Perhaps
almost the way I felt when I dove into the ocean; but this
was less freeing and more frightening. My left hand was

going to be numb by the time we landed; it was holding onto the armrest so tightly.

"You don't have to be so afraid, Summer. You act as if you've never been on a plane before," she said with a smile, patting my right hand. She had flown much more often than I had in my own lifetime. I gave her a small smile, trying to hold in my anxiety. I wanted the plane ride to be over. I wanted to be on the ground already.

I hadn't realized that I was holding my breath until the plane suddenly touched land. My fingers were red from my grasp on the chair handles and felt sore as I released them and tried to flex them. My fingers felt as if they had forgotten how to bend and move and work properly. I wondered how many flights we'd take after this to go home. I wasn't sure I'd have fingers left. We weren't even off the plane when my mother had her cell phone to her ear. After a few "okays" and a "ciao," she turned to me with a smile.

"Your father is waiting for us next to the luggage carousels." She seemed happier about it than I was. I just wanted to get back on the plane and fly back home. I looked out the window one last time before we stood up to leave. Greece was waiting for me. It was full of browns and greens and vast blue sky. It seemed so different than my ocean world with lighthouses and fishing boats. I wasn't sure how I felt about this vast change of surroundings.

My father's face was a lot tanner than I remembered it, but it was still the same kind face that I looked forward to seeing since my arrival home.

"How's my little artist?" he asked as he wrapped his tan arms around me. I must have looked like a ghost in his arms. I gave him a warm smile as I pushed my bangs out of my face as I pulled away.

"I'm shocked I'm actually here."

"I know! I know…" He started, although his voice said otherwise. He wasn't sharing the same emotions that I was feeling. He wasn't shocked. He was probably more in a hurry to get us home, so he could show us all the things we were missing while he was alone in Greece. He reached out for my mother and gently kissed her cheek and brushed a strand of her blonde hair out of her face.

"This was a shock to me too when I was offered the job, but you knew that. It's going to be great." He directed us toward the luggage carousel. Suitcases and bags were rotating around and around. It was almost as if everyone was flaunting their dirty laundry: the things we all travel with.

"How was the flight?" My father asked, helping me pull my heavy purple suitcase. I was the only one there with such an outrageous color. I liked it that way.

"Pretty smooth," my mother grunted as she grabbed her oversized black suitcase. It was the exact size of her, and I wondered if she'd sent her clothes over in boxes the way I had. Was everything that she needed right in there? My father leaned over to help my mother heave her suitcase next to her. He laughed, shaking his head.

"You never change. Always packing the whole house."

"This time, you told us to," she said matter-of-factly, jabbing her finger into his shoulder with a bright smile of her own. It was as if my parents were two completely different people when they were out of the house and together. They were about to pursue their dream job together, the one thing that the two of them loved to do together. I knew I was going to be the one who would get left behind at the house. I could see my mother and father on trips together, or out on sites for long hours, and I'd be left in our new home. And this time, I had no place to claim as my own.

My father walked us to his white rent-a-car Suzuki and pushed our entire luggage into the back seats next to me. My mother's suitcase took up most of the room, and I almost felt like I was sitting on it. I tried to push the seat belt into the buckle, but the luggage was in the way. I kept it around me with my hands instead and tried to hold it in place.

"All set?" My dad asked, glancing back at me with a warm smile. I must have looked ridiculous surrounded by our entire luggage. I gave him a small nod, and my mother clapped her hands together. She was more than ready. She reminded me of an animated character in Disney that was all too enthusiastic about adventure.

"Show us Athens, honey." She acted as if she had never seen Athens before. There had been plenty of trips to Athens that the two of them took. It was still the same as it was a few years ago, minus the few local stores that might have opened or closed, and perhaps there were new roadways.

"Are you two hungry? Did you get something on the plane?"

I wanted to tell him what a joke the food was on the plane. Even the TV dinners that were in the fridge back at home were better than what they tried to serve my mother and me. My mother looked at him with urgency, as if she hadn't eaten a huge sandwich in the airport in London, or snacked on a huge bag of potato chips in the waiting area back in Rhode Island. I couldn't stomach anything that early in the morning the way she could.

"Yes. We are," my mother spoke up before I could tell him that all I truly wanted to do was sleep. I caught my dad's eyes in the review mirror, and I gave him a shrug.

He patted my mother's leg and nodded. "All right, we'll stop at a little place on the way home," he glanced at me again through the mirror. "It's a quick little place."

I let my head fall back onto the car headrest and closed my eyes. The Greek sun fought to open my eyes, giving me a show behind my eyelids of bright orange and yellow. It was almost as if I were looking through a kaleidoscope, all with my eyes closed. It was a painting with round balls that were coated with different colors, meshing and rolling around, making a design that was new and fresh. I hadn't done a painting like that since grade school. Here it was, on display in my own mind. It was like opening a whole new world that I was sinking into. The colors became places, and soon, my feet were back in the ocean sand.

I knew I was dreaming, and I didn't want to wake up. I pushed myself further into the colors; the sand becoming a green that was the grass at school. My classmates' faces smiling at me with paint smudged on their cheeks. The colors became my emotions – the fear I felt inside. A new start. *Greece. Him.* Then there was black. *Night.* There was the sand again, and I was painting him as he stood in front of me. He was like a dream. *His black hair, his pale skin, and his dark eyes.* Those eyes that I loved. The eyes that I knew could see something in me that I could not. The lips that I imagined were on mine. My mind was racing. My heart was beating so fast. My hands worked as I tried to stop them. His hand reached out to me; the white of his fingers grazed my skin and then I was in his arms. There was no sound. No paint. Just the smell of ocean salt and dirt and him and in his hand was a ripe, red pomegranate. My mouth watered at the sight and I was reaching for it. I knew the taste of forever.

"Oh my god!" I heard my mother shouting through my dream, and I tried to stay. I fought my way to stay in the dream, but I felt his hands drift away, and the black became the interior of the car as my eyes opened, and darted to my mother. She was all the way back in her seat, and my father's voice was shouting.

Time stopped at that moment. Everything happened in slow motion. My mind couldn't keep up. The car pushed to the left, and I saw a car moving right toward us. There was nothing my father could do. The car slammed into us, pushing our bodies back into our seats. My parents' bodies looked like rag dolls as they bounced around, slamming into the windows and each other. Then suddenly there was another slam. My body bent and my head slammed into the side window. There was pain. I could only focus on the pain. There was no sound. I waited to hear my mother. I wanted to hear, "everything will be okay," but there was nothing.

I closed my eyes, waiting for another impact, and I tried to wake myself up. I wanted to believe that all of this was a dream. I would wake up, and my father would be pulling into a tiny villa, where we'd get some of my mother's favorite food, and I would be happy at the house my father had for us. I wanted to know that this was just a part of the dream, and I could wake up from it. I felt the car move again; I guess another car had hit us, and suddenly everything was upside down. I couldn't figure which way was up. The suffocation in my lungs caused me to believe that I was truly drowning; falling, tumbling over myself and everything in the back seat of the car tumbling with me. *Falling.* I couldn't catch my breath. I was lost in an ocean of glass, metal, and blood. Then there was darkness, and I didn't know how to get away. I was stuck in the tangle of the seatbelt that was wrapped around my arm. The only sounds I could hear were of my panicked breathing. I couldn't stop. I knew with one look at my parents, their still forms hovered over the bloody airbags, I was either alone or dead myself.

Was this what it felt like when you died?

Chapter Seven

My eyes hurt. It felt like someone had punched me
several times in the face. I wanted to move, but my legs felt
as if there were several needles prickling into my skin and
feet in all the worst places. I felt the needles in my hands. I
hate needles. My mind raced. Where was I? Was I still in
the car? Where were my parents? A flash of their faces
flickered through my mind. *The airport. Their smiles. My
father's eyes in the rearview mirror.* There was a pain in
my heart that made me want to scream. The memory of
their still forms over the airbags haunted me. I knew the
answer already. I knew they were dead. I was the only one
alive. I was lost in a foreign country with no family. I'd
never get back home. I wanted to die. I should have died
with them.

"She's mine." There was a voice in the room with me.
It was faint, and it seemed to pull me out of the aftermath
of the dream I was having. I wondered if it was just a part
of my mind.

"I'm sorry Κύριε; you gave us no identification. How
can we know you are who you say you are?" It was a
woman. Not my mother. A warm and comforting hand
touched my arm, and fixed the cloth that was wrapped
around my feet. I wondered if the warm hand belonged to
the woman's voice. I wondered if she knew I had no
family. That I was alone with nothing. No dreams, no
parents, no future.

"I just flew all the way from the United States to
collect my niece. You will not give me a hard time." The
male voice said more strongly and forcefully. I should have

opened my eyes then. I should have called out the imposter. Whoever this was, he had the wrong girl. I had no Uncles. I had no one.

"Can you show identification?" she tried again, and this time, the male grunted. It sounded like he was trying to pull something from his clothing.

"Here," he growled. There was silence. I felt myself drifting back to sleep. I knew this had to be all in my head. If I fell back asleep, would he be waiting for me? Would I go back to the ocean and feel the sun's rays on my face? Would I die there?

"She's too weak to leave." The woman stated. It was a fact. I tried to lift my finger, but there was nothing. My body didn't want to function. It was too painful. I could only dig my fingertips into what I imagined as the white, crisp hospital blankets that I always saw in movies.

"She needs to come home and get better there."

"I can only recommend that she stay here for a few more days."

"I want the doctor to release her today. I have two tickets for flights to go back to America tomorrow morning."

"I cannot do that. I refuse." Her warm hands were gone, and I could only listen. I heard shuffling and then his harsh voice. I could only imagine what he was doing, whoever this stranger was.

"I will not leave without her. You either get the release forms, or I'll just take her now. Hell, I'll have her sign herself out."

"You cannot," she muttered.

"Watch me." He snapped, and I heard the clamor of shoes walking toward my bed. I forced my eyes to open, and his face was there. I knew his face. I knew who he was. His eyes met mine, and they were full of anger. His black hair flowed down past his shoulders, and he was dressed in black. He looked so different from the times on the beach. He didn't look unusual and enchanted. He looked normal. The kind of normal that only existed in magazines.

"Do not touch her!" the woman tried to grab his shoulder, but he and I both knew that she didn't stand a chance. He would always be stronger and cleverer than anyone else. If he wanted me, he would have me. In my state, I knew I wouldn't win. His voice felt warm, as his pale hands reached for my needle infested one.

"You know our agreement. Do you wish to come with me?"

I had nowhere to go. I had no one to claim me. He was here, and he was willing to take me. The way I was. I didn't know what would happen to me if I didn't take him up on his offer now. If I refused, I knew that one day soon, he'd come anyway, and he'd be ready for the struggle. He pushed the woman off of him, and he turned back to me.

"Summer. Let me take you home."

"I have no home. It died with them," I whispered.

He lifted my hand to his lips, and he shook his head. "No. It didn't. You still have a home with me." There was some sort of truth in his voice that I knew had to be real. I knew that he wasn't lying to me. He could be a home to me; whatever home was now. My Dad and Mom were dead. All things that had been home were gone. He could be the person that I could trust, for now. I had trusted the idea of him for so long. Why wouldn't I just trust the real thing? I closed my eyes, lowering my head back down onto the pillow. My head started to feel heavy and full of pain. The kind of pain that made me imagine a beating heart locked inside of my brain; pulsing and pushing, and I wanted to tell him to go away.

"Let me take you home," he whispered again. I felt his cool lips on my knuckles and slowly I felt a needle slip out of my skin. One by one, he took each needle out of my hands, and arms. I opened my eyes and saw we were the only ones in the room. The woman was gone. I wondered if she had run for security.

"We only have a few minutes. If you want to go with me, we have to go now," he whispered, knowing what I was thinking. He turned back toward a brown, leather chair that was in the corner of the hospital room. I took a moment to glance at the crème colored walls with the flowery wallpaper that went around the middle. There were fake paintings of flowers that I could only guess were manufactured by machines to create thousands of paintings that looked the same.

"I grabbed these for you," he said, pushing a pair of my jeans and a t-shirt my way. "I grabbed some undergarments as well. They're rolled up in your shirt." He pointed at the t-shirt, and I felt my cheeks get warm.

"Where is my stuff?" I glanced around the room, looking for a brush or a toothbrush.

"In the car I'm renting." I looked at him confused. If he was a God, why was he renting a car?

"I have to look normal, Summer. I have to play the part," he said, lifting his hands in a quote gesture. It felt odd to me to watch him try to be normal, when he was so far from being such.

"What name are you going by?" I asked softly. My voice was still faint. My throat still hurt. He glanced down at his identification card and smiled. His lips were pinker, more human.

"Alec."

"So, I have to call you Uncle Alec?"

"Until we're in the car," he murmured, pulling the curtain in front of him. It was my queue to get dressed. I stared at my clothing. My hands felt helpless. How was I going to move fast enough for him?

"Do you need help?" he whispered, peering from behind the curtain for a moment. My eyes filled with embarrassed and upset tears, though, it was all I could do to keep them in. I pushed my weak hands up to my face and tried to count backwards, hoping it would calm me. I couldn't break down here. I couldn't let him see. His hands pulled at my wrists as he lifted my chin gently with his finger. He wiped a tear that fell down my cheek and lifted the shirt that was beside him.

"I promise you can cry as much as you want in the car," he whispered, and quickly began to untie the knots to my hospital gown. His hands moved so fast that I didn't have a chance to object.

"I won't look, if that's what you're worried about," he pressed, continuing his routine of clothing me. My shirt was on in no time, and then followed my jeans. Before I knew it, he was tying my shoelaces and gently picked me up in his arms.

"You don't have to carry me," I murmured, trying to push at his chest, but I knew my weak arms had no fight left in them.

"Just relax," he whispered into my hair. "Rest your head and close your eyes. You're safe."

I knew I should believe him, so I did. I laid my head on his shoulder, pushing his black hair to the side and closed my eyes.

"Where do you think you're going?" I heard a male voice try to stop us, but he continued to walk.

"You can't just take her out of here like this. She needs medical attention." This voice belonged to the woman who had been in the room with me earlier. She must have tried to get help.

"She's fine. She needs to come home with me," he murmured. I could hear the sound of his voice vibrate throughout his chest. It was a comforting feeling. It reminded me of times when I had cried, and my father had picked me up, wrapping me in his arms. I could hear his breath – the comforting way his voice soothed me. I fought tears. I felt my grip tighten around his neck, and he began to walk again, this time, faster.

"We're almost there, Summer," he soothed, tightening his grip on me.

"Will we get out?"

"Trust me," he said with a deep sigh. "We will."

Another staff member stopped him, but he didn't falter. "She belongs to me," he murmured, and tried to walk past, but the man in scrubs pushed him and tried to knock me out of his arms. I opened my eyes and stared at the man. I knew we'd have trouble until I finally said something.

67

"I want to go with him." My words felt so ultimate. I finally said the one thing he wanted to hear. I knew it was what he was waiting for. He walked past the man and down the hallway. He and I didn't speak a word. He seemed to nearly just walk out of the hospital with me in his arms without anyone else stopping him. He gently put me down when we reached a car door of some silver vehicle I couldn't make out or recognize. He opened the door and watched as I stared at the seat. A flash of my family and me in the car flickered across my memory; my mother's enthusiasm to eat, my father's tan face, his gentle eyes meeting mine. The tears that I had been trying so hard to fight were falling down my cheeks. My heart ached. I'd never see them again. I'd never hear their voices again. And how could he just expect me to hop into another car after the accident?

"Do you trust me, Summer?"

I glanced back at him for a moment and then at the car.

"You're immortal. You can't die. What if you forget the fact that I can?" I could easily die in another car accident. I didn't understand why I hadn't died with my family. I should have.

"Are you scared?" *Of dying?* Yes. I was. The flash of my parents in my head made the fear more alive – more alarming. "I'll drive carefully. I promise." He responded gently as if he had read my mind.

That wasn't good enough for me. I stood there longer, looking for the strength to get into the car. I wanted to pretend that nothing bad happened, but the sting of pain and death were too strong. My body was throbbing from standing, and I finally gave in and pushed myself into the car seat. The ache of my body and my heart finally let loose and tears filled my eyes again. This time, there was nothing that could stop them.

He closed the door behind me and made his way into the driver's seat. He leaned over me to clip my seat belt into place and then he started the engine and began our journey away from the hospital. My tears blurred my vision of Athens and the traffic around me. I leaned my head against the cold window and tried to think of anything that could end the pain. My father and mother were never going to come back. My home in Point Judith was gone. My school, my beach, and my whole everything was gone. Just gone.

"Where are we going?" I whispered, trying to push my tears back and away. They could wait until later. They had to wait until later. "Are we really going to America tomorrow?"

"No." His voice was harsh again. "We're going to a hotel for now. From there, we'll decide."

"Aren't you going to take me to where you live?" There was a long moment of silence. I thought he hadn't heard me.

"Eventually, yes," he murmured, finally. "We'll be at the hotel in ten minutes, so just rest." I felt his cool hand on my leg, and I did what he told me to do.

It was hard to fight sleep at this point; my body felt tired and worn out. I wanted to curl up into a ball and give in to the wave of slumber. It wasn't too long until I felt myself fall deep into the blackness of sleep. There was only a white canvas and I. The canvas began to melt as if hot water poured all over it, and it began to show the painting that had been in the kitchen. It was Persephone and Demeter. This time, Demeter wasn't picking a rose from the rose bush. Her hand was extended to Persephone, holding a large cup. I could almost hear her speaking; her soft voice taunting her daughter. 'Drink!' it said, over and over again. 'Drink and be free.' Be free of what? I touched the painting and tried to stop the scene, but my hand soaked right into the canvas. I was falling. I was falling right into the scene. The colors were rushing around me, and I couldn't breathe. The cup was in front of me, and my mother's face taunted me – sneered at me. 'Drink and be free of it all.' And then his hands were on me, all over me. Pulling me back, pushing me down, and shaking me.

"Summer! Wake up!" His voice shot through me like a lightning bolt, and my eyes opened wide.

"It was just a dream," he whispered, brushing his hand across my cheek. His black hair fell into his face, and I had the desire to push it away. I wanted to feel his hair in my hands. Would that make him more real? Is he just a part of my imagination too?

"You're safe with me. I promise." I was shaking, and I noticed my hand was gripping his arm. I let go of him and gently fell back into the car seat. The seatbelt was digging into my neck, and I unbuckled it, noticing we were parked in front of a very elaborate hotel building. Each balcony had a different color painted on the walls and ceiling.

"Are we in art heaven?" I whispered, glancing out of the windshield of the car. He gave me a gentle laugh and touched my forehead.

"You really think you're dead, don't you?"

"I should be," I whispered, glancing down at my hands. They looked as if I had fallen off a bicycle and landed on the pavement. They hurt like that too.

"Let's just get you inside, and you can rest," he whispered, giving me a warm smile that seemed to push me enough to open the car door on my own. He was there in an instant to pick me up and carry me into the hotel.

Chapter Eight

I hadn't ever imagined a claw foot bathtub to be comfortable or even large enough to move around in, but the one in the suite that he booked for us was more than I ever imagined. It was stainless white, and I could almost lay completely flat in it. The water felt good on my sore skin. I looked down at my arms and saw deep blue and purple bruises, the same kinds that I had imagined on the beach days ago. How long had that been? How long had I been asleep in the hospital? What happened to my parents' bodies? I tried to rub away the residue of my sadness with the hot water all over my face. I couldn't think about them. I wanted to push the sadness away and focus on getting better. My skin was wrinkly already, but I didn't want to get out. I leaned over carefully, trying to avoid my sore bones as I turned the red lever, letting the bath heat up with fresh hot water.

"How many times are you going to do that tonight? Aren't you done?" I heard his voice call from the bedroom. I wanted to ignore his presence, but it was almost inescapable.

"I just don't want to get out yet," I called back, turning off the lever and pushing myself back against the tub wall. I knew I had to get out soon. I would fall asleep and would most likely drown in this tub if I stayed any longer.

"Do you need help getting out?" As embarrassing as the idea was, I knew he was only offering because of how weak I was.

"Can you help me with your eyes closed?" I murmured underneath my breath.

There was a faint knock on the door that startled me, and I looked around for the closest towel. I left it on the sink counter. Go me.

"I promise I'll keep my eyes closed," I heard him say. I held my breath as the door opened and a burst of cold air rushed into the room. It made me want to sink down below into the hot water and stay there. He reached for the towel that was on the sink counter, and he turned toward me. His eyes were closed, and he reached out, extending the towel in my direction.

"Wrap that around yourself and I'll get you a dry towel if that gets too wet."

I slowly tried to stand, wrapping the white warmth around me and grabbing his shoulder as he helped to lift me from the bath.

"Where are my clothes?"

"I left them in the bedroom, waiting for you."

"I won't need help with them," I said with a smile. He opened his eyes for a moment, keeping his gaze locked on mine.

"I only want to help you, Summer. I know the pain you must be going through…" His handsomeness still took my breath away. He didn't look at all the same from what I remembered on the beach. His black cloak was gone; his stringy hair wasn't so stark and stringy; the way it had been on the beach. He looked like he blended into the culture here, as if he were destined to live among people all the time. He probably could. His eyes seemed more human, and yet still so familiar. I knew the curve of those eyes, the color and the hidden messages locked away in them. Just as I knew everything else about him. He wasn't a stranger to me at all. I shouldn't have been so embarrassed or cautious around him. He knew me better than anyone else.

He walked me into the bedroom and helped me sit down on the corner of the white bedspread. Everything was white and edgy. There were only hints of subtle color around the room. It wasn't as much of an art heaven as I had imagined from the outside. Beside me were my clothes that I gently rolled up in Point Judith. There were tiny creases that I tried to smooth with my fingers, but I eventually gave up and slipped the clothes on while he went back into the bathroom to let the bathwater out.

His kindness toward me resurfaced the tears that I was trying so hard to keep down. I couldn't stop them as they slipped over onto my cheeks. The only thing I could think to do was crawl into the white bed and envelope myself in the blankets. My every thought was of my parents. The last image I saw of them in the car. Bloody. *Dead. Our home at the beach. The kitchen.* Our good times there at the kitchen table. The rainy days that kept us inside and I would paint. I'd bring them a new painting to hang up on the walls in the living room. *My father's face.* He was so warm, so kind. I closed my eyes, bringing the memories more to life. I could see everything like a movie. My father greeting us at the airport, pushing us into the car, and then suddenly, they were both gone. Everything was gone. I felt so disconnected and alone. I had no real place to call my own anymore.

The bed shifted and soon followed his arm, which wrapped around me; he was holding me. "You shouldn't cry, Summer."

"I just lost my parents. I have every right to cry," I choked out.

He didn't say anything. I felt him let out a heavy sigh, and he held me tighter against himself. I could feel his hard chest on my back. "I wish I had the right words to comfort you."

I probably wouldn't have let him be so close to me, or even be comfortable enough to let him touch me this way if we were still in Rhode Island. I would have pushed him away, struggled, and screamed. Anything to get him away from me. Now, I couldn't get enough of the physical contact. I needed to be held. I needed a person to tell me that life didn't end with just death. There was more to it than that. He was the perfect person to say the words. He lived it. He was the King of the Dead. He was my God of Death. I peered down at his pale arms folded around my waist and pulled his hand toward mine. I realized I didn't even have a name for him. I didn't even know what to call him.

"I don't even know what name to call you," I whispered, scanning over the hundreds of Greeks Gods and Goddesses' names. Hades was unique, but not something that I could call him out loud. It was still strange to me, to know that the man I had read about in stories was lying on the same bed with me.

"I don't really have another name," he murmured. "But I suppose you can call me whatever you like if it pleases you to do so." The name from his identification card echoed in my head as I drew over the creases in the palm of his hand.

"So if I wanted to just name you something, you wouldn't be upset?"

"Why would I?" he questioned, pulling his hand away from mine.

"Because you're Hades. That's your name," I said, slowly turning over to face him. It hurt so much to move.

"It's who I am. It's a name that was bestowed on me, but it is not what I choose to be called," he whispered, lifting the blankets to make my move easier.

"What do the others call you?" I asked as he tucked the blankets around me and I rested my head close to his.

"Others?" His dark eyebrows lifted, and his eyes were clouded with names and faces that I probably only ever read about it books.

"I know that if you're real, the others have to be real. What do the others call you? What does Persephone call you?"

There was a long moment of silence. I knew I had to have hit a sore spot when I mentioned her name. His eyes glared into mine for a few minutes, and I saw his jaw tighten.

"The others address me as Lord, Sire…" His voice drifted into a whisper, and he turned onto his back, putting more distance between us.

"And what about her? Does she even know you're here?" I asked as I lifted my head up to look into his face. He closed his eyes and pursed his lips.

"You should sleep, Summer." His voice was hard and full of anger and hurt.

"Tell me about her." I pressed on. He ignored me. He lay on the bed so still that I couldn't see his chest rising with each breath. I pushed his shoulder, trying to get his attention. I wanted to get an answer from him. "Why won't you answer? Why won't you mention her?"

"Why don't you just give up? I don't wish to speak about her," he snapped, his eyes opening and exposing the red fire of anger that I had never imagined I'd see in him.

"I just want to know more," I murmured, tucking my hair behind my ear.

"You don't even know who you are, do you?" he said angrily, pushing himself off the bed and whirled around to look at me. "I really thought that my presence would be a huge clue to you, Summer. I don't just show up in front of *anybody*." I watched him as he paced in front of the bed, and I wanted to reach out to him and apologize. I wasn't sure what to say.

"Once you're strong enough to go, we'll go to my home. You'll see then. You'll understand why I'm here."

"Then take me. You already have me here. I have nowhere else to go. No one knows where I am, or who you are. If you wanted to succeed in a kidnapping, you did it *again*."

"I didn't kidnap you!" He shouted, pounding his fist down on the white comforter. The bed shook. My heart raced. I was getting angry listening to him. I wanted to stand up and shout till I couldn't anymore, but I wasn't strong enough. My head was pounding with pain, and I wanted to get up and go outside. I wanted fresh air.

"You said that you wanted to go with me," he said, pointing his finger at me. "You said it."

"And you said that in a month's time, I wouldn't have any choice anyway. Either way, you win. I'm here, aren't

I? I should have stayed in the hospital. Look at me! I can't even stand up! I can't get dressed by myself. I'm solely dependent on you, but that's how you wanted it, isn't it? I bet you even planned my parents' death." The truth of my words flew out of my mouth before I could stop them. I didn't know where it came from, but I knew I was right. He said that everything would be taken care of when I mentioned my parents in the past. He planned the only thing he knew how to plan. *Death.*

"That's right. You had one month," he repeated, giving me an angry nod.

"That month is almost over!" I shouted and felt my eyes cloud with tears. Angry hot tears. "I wasn't given any other choice but to go with you. What would have become of me if I stayed? Become a ward of the country? Get shipped back to America with nothing? You were the only card I had left."

"If you're trying to politely say that you used me, I don't care," he snarled. "You're right. You're here now. And I won't let you go. You belong to me. You always have. You always will. I don't care if you don't understand why or not. Just accept it." His words were final.

I pushed the blankets out of my way and grabbed the softest pillow from the bed I could find. He looked at me confused as I limped toward the bathroom with a pillow in my hand. The tub would be my bed tonight.

Chapter Nine

There was a knock on the bathroom door, but I ignored it. The door was locked. There was no way he was going to get inside unless he pulled a God move that magically opened the door. I was situated in the tub with towels from the closet, making my own creation of a bed.

"You can sleep on the bed, Summer." I heard his muffled voice from the other side of the door.

"If you think I want to be anywhere near you, you have something else coming," I mumbled underneath my breath.

"Let me in so we can talk," He said it more like he was giving me an order, rather than a choice.

"I can't get up to unlock the door." I hoped that would work, and he'd leave me alone. I tucked stray locks of my brown hair gently behind my ears. They even felt bruised. I looked down at the shadows of my hands and wondered how they looked now. Were they as bruised as they had been hours before? Was there some magical way that he could cure me, and I'd be healed? I wouldn't want the pain to go away, even if he could cure me. It was the only thing that kept me alive. It was the only thing that was different between my parents and me. I was alive to feel the pain.

The click of the lock startled me, and I heard the door open slowly.

"Should I close my eyes?"

I didn't answer. I heard his shoes on the tiled floor come closer and closer until he was looming over the tub. The fear that I had felt before, only weeks ago, filled my chest. His black hair and black clothes blended in with the darkness. Only his pale skin and shining eyes stood out to me the most. I turned my head away from him, back toward the side of the tub. There was a silent chill that ran down my spine. It felt the same as when we first met. He was chilling; a piece of my nightmare that came to life. Here I was, lying in a tub in front of the Death God, and my only protection was a towel.

"Summer." His voice was so close to my ear, yet I didn't turn toward him. I curled my knees to my chest and buried my face deeper into the stark white pillow. "Please don't turn away."

I kept my lips closed. I didn't look at him. I felt his hand on my shoulder, and he gently pulled me toward him. I didn't put up a fight. I was too sore. Too uncomfortable. I couldn't see his face clearly. He was a mesh of black and shadows.

"I'm sorry."

His words surprised me, and I pushed myself up so that I was sitting. "Did you plan my parents' death?"

There was silence. I could hear the people above us walk around, the pump of water, the television from the room next to us. Everything but him. I reached out for any part of him. I couldn't see. I felt the skin that my fingers touched and knew it was his face. It was smooth and soft. There wasn't any stubble on his cheek. It was exactly the way I knew it would be. The way I imagined it.

"Did you kill my parents?"

"I didn't," he whispered. It was soft and sad. "I'm on your side, Summer. I promise. I wouldn't do anything to hurt you."

"But you'd do anything to keep me."

"Yes," he whispered. "Anything to have you and keep you." Another shiver went down my spine. I knew that I should have been scared, worried even. But I wasn't.

"Will you come to bed now?" He asked, lifting me by my hands until I stood up in the white tub.

I supposed I didn't have any choice. He lifted me into his arms without a sound and walked me back into the bedroom, where he gently placed me in the bed. I could only watch him in amazement as he pulled the blankets over me and stood there for a moment. His eyes caught mine. The simple glimmer of his spoke thousands of words to me. He was telling me the truth. He wanted me safe. He wanted me with him. He wanted that to be enough. He pulled away and strolled to the white chair in the corner of the room, where he sat quietly for what felt like hours. My eyes tried to fight sleep, but eventually, I lost.

* * * *

"Get out of bed, we're going out," he said as he leaned over the black television and turned it off. I glared at him and clicked the power back on. The news lady was saying something in Greek, but it was a better distraction then silence. Anything was better than silence.

"I'm serious. We're going out," he repeated as he again, leaned over and turned off the power button. He turned back to me just as I raised my arm to turn the television back on.

"Don't you even think about it. I won't let you just mope around in bed all week."

"I'm tired," I grumbled, piling the covers over my head and lying flat on my stomach. I didn't want to get out of bed. I didn't want to face the day, the city, or the reality. I didn't want to do anything.

"I look like a beaten wife."

"If that's the case, then I'm the one who has to worry, not you," he teased, pulling back the covers and pulling my hand until I was practically out of bed. He opened the nearby closet and started to rummage through my luggage.

"You know, you really shouldn't do that. Those are my clothes."

"Well, you seem pretty incompetent, so I have to do something," he said as he pulled out a pair of my jeans and a light purple t-shirt. "Get dressed."

I glared at him as I stood up and jerked the clothes out of his hand. He had a smirk on his face as I pushed past him and went into the white bathroom. My towels from the night before were neatly folded up over the side of the tub. I could picture him coming in here and taking the time to put the bathroom back into place. Hades was a neat freak.

"Where do you want to go so badly?" I asked as I squeezed toothpaste onto my green toothbrush and looked at myself in the mirror. My hair was disheveled, and I tried to pull through my tangles with my fingers. I had dark circles under my eyes and I still had a large scratch on my forehead. I glanced down at my hands and noticed the dark purple bruises on my arms. It looked as if someone had pulled me out by my arms; there were finger bruises everywhere. I pushed the toothbrush into my mouth and scrubbed my teeth until the morning aftertaste was gone. When I glanced back up at the mirror, I saw him standing in the doorway.

"Don't you knock?"

"Do you want to do some sightseeing?"

"I've seen everything in Greece already," I grumbled, as I put my toothbrush down on the counter and exchanged it for the blue brush that the hotel offered. I tried to brush through my tangles as carefully as I could. My brown hair didn't want to cooperate.

"You've already seen everything? Is that even possible?" He looked surprised, or maybe only half surprised.

"You forget that I've been coming here since I was a child. My dad came here a lot to do excavations."

"So I guess Agora or Acropolis has already been seen?"

"Mostly," I lied. My mother had always been about avoiding places like that when it came to trips to Athens. She was jealous that my father could go dig and discover, but she couldn't. She was stuck with me. She'd dress me up and take me shopping through Athens' malls and museums. I'd at least seen the museums over twenty times.

"Well, it's been a while since I've seen them. We're going there," he said. Reaching for the doorknob, he closed the door. I sighed, grabbing my jeans and the shirt and wished, hoped the day would go fast. I really wanted nothing more than to curl back up in bed and pretend that everything around me wasn't real, and I was indeed dead.

Agora was exactly the way I remembered it. Rubble and stone in shapes of old structures and temples. I could imagine my father digging around the bricks and columns, the faces of time and history. It was places like this that were the setting of so many stories about the Gods and Goddesses that used to litter our house. Instead of pictures that were framed on our walls and shelves, I was standing in front of the real thing. . I felt lost in a world of color and time and a place that I'd never know but always fantasize about. I finally understood what it was that my mother longed for in this place: It was the history and the love, the passion that these people had to make their beliefs come to life. To the Greeks, their Gods were real, walking, breathing people, and as I turned to look at Hades, I realized the power of their faith. He was real, walking, talking, and breathing.

"You look a little overwhelmed," he whispered into my ear as he leaned towards me, grabbing my hand to get me out of the way of a walking tourist. I turned my gaze up towards him and gave him a half smile. I was still completely lost in my own thoughts.

"I'm just thinking."

Hades looked a little curious, smirking and bumping his shoulder against mine. For a moment, he truly looked like a normal man. I wondered what we looked like to the others surrounding us.

"What are you thinking about?" he asked, turning his eyes towards the broken stones in front of us.

"Just that it's really, very beautiful here." The trees were large and vibrant. The branches seemed to stretch out like arms, worshiping the timeless columns in their own way. This place was the foundation for all the stories that I had grown up with. Each stone was a story; a handprint of a piece of time. The sky was blue lapis and made everything else seem more than just real, but alive.

"I thought you said you had been here before," he commented as I let out a sigh.

"Not to this place."

"So, I guess you haven't seen the temples up close then?"

He was testing me. How devoted had I been? How devoted had my parents been? I could see the picture of the two of them, the younger versions of themselves standing in front of a temple in the kitchen. They had gone to see many temples before I was born. They had been on digs and discovered objects together.

"Your silence means that you haven't," he laughed and pulled me in the direction of dozens of large columns. They seemed to emerge from the ground like trees. Large parts of the earth that couldn't stand to be confound to the ground. With the sun high in the sky, I could feel the sweat rolling down my back. I tried to picture a time when these columns were parts of thriving houses, temples, structures that meant more than just the discovery of history. What these structures represented had been the way of life for the Ancient Greeks.

"You do know of Zeus, right? Your parents did, at least, cover that much with you?" he asked half jokingly. I knew he had to be joking. I glared at him and bit the inside of my cheek.

"Of course, I do. Of course, they did," I snapped. He didn't falter. Instead, he simply pointed towards thirteen tall pillars in the distance.

"That is all that's left of my brother's temple," he whispered with a glint of happiness in his voice. It was almost as if he was satisfied that there was nothing left of his arch nemesis. How could it be that his brothers, all of them, were against one another? I stared at him, watching as his jaw clenched, a millennia of anger building up inside of him. If there had ever been a moment that I had doubted this man and his accusation that he was Hades, it was gone the moment I heard the clip of happiness in his words. He detested Zeus; just the way all the stories told. The rivalry between them was much deeper than simply who had a bigger temple than the other. Hades felt as if his own brother had betrayed him. I grabbed his hand hesitantly, unsure how he'd react. Would he pull away? His gaze wavered down to our joined hands and slowly, eased up to meet my own. I pulled him away from the stones gently.

"We have better things to see," I murmured under my breath, pulling him towards anything else but that place. I didn't want to see him get angry over something he could not change; something far greater than himself.

"I'm sorry," he grumbled, pulling his other hand through his dark locks and turned his gaze away from me. For being a God, he was really sensitive, and it really surprised me, and yet, I wasn't. There was something about him that I knew, or understood to be dark and lonely. I wondered what Zeus was really like. Was he the way our society made him out to be? I knew for certain that Zeus was known for liking his women, and supplied the earth with plenty of children. My father tried to make a joke about him after reading several stories of his affairs, but it turned out to just be awful.

"If Zeus said, 'whose your daddy?' *everyone* would say 'you are!'" my father laughed as he put the book of Greek Mythology down on the glass coffee table in our living room. I had been sitting on my father's lap, listening to him read me the many stories that he loved when he had

86

chosen to share his new joke. I couldn't recall anyone laughing but himself. I had brought up that many of the characters either were children of Zeus or were almost directly linked and he grinned, proud of himself for making such a terrible joke. My mother hated that joke and always warned him that Zeus was watching. My father would go after my mother and press a soft kiss against her cheek and tell her that he already knew he was forgiven: her love would protect him. She'd always give him a look that said otherwise, but he was none-the-wiser. Perhaps it was that her love couldn't protect him from his own terrible jokes.

"Can I ask you a question?" I asked the God at my side, lifting my hand over my eyes to shield them from the bright sun. He nodded and stopped, lifting his hand over my face to help me.

"What is he like?"

"Zeus?" he questioned, raising his eyebrow curiously at me.

"Yes, Zeus," I murmured. He stood there, puzzled for a moment.

"It's been a while since I've seen him. And you can imagine the reason why I don't get a lot of visitors," he said, his eyes shifting around nervously. I could tell he was trying to collect his thoughts. It was an odd feeling to hear him speak so freely and openly about people who had always been characters in books to me. They were real; just as real as he was. Every story that I ever read was based on real events. These Gods weren't just figments of the Greek's imaginations. They were *real*. I wondered if the Greeks knew that. They must have known the truth. Had the Gods shown themselves to them at one point or another? Did they tell them of things to come? How to worship them? I glanced at Hades in front of me; I had spent the day watching him closely, carefully; his jaw clenching, the way his gaze locked onto mine, the way his lips turned into a slight smirk when he knew he had the upper hand. He was flawless in the way he moved and spoke, despite his odd and dark presence. The world suddenly seemed complete; he was the balance to everything. Life and death. He looked as if he had come out of a movie. I hadn't noticed how flawless— how perfect he looked until now. The people around me must have wondered what on earth he was doing with a normal girl like me. His eyes looked into mine as if he could read every thought, every image that I was thinking.

"Are you alright, Summer?" He touched my face, and I held my breath, watching his eyes search mine. What was wrong with me? I wanted to push him away and tell him to leave me alone, to not touch me. But I couldn't resist. He was too beautiful, too kind. He was the man that I had been fantasizing about for years. I knew him, no matter what lie I told myself.

"I'm fine," I whispered, pushing his hand off of my face and I started to walk away when his hand caught my arm carefully.

"I know this is a lot to take in. I understand."

"You can't understand. You've always been this way."

"There's going to be more to take in, Summer. When the time is right, you're going to find out so much more about yourself, and life and the truth about everything."

"I don't want to talk about this," I murmured, yanking my arm out of his grasp. "Not unless you just tell me what I do not understand." I watched him shake his head, and he began to walk beside me.

"I can't tell you anything, Summer. The discovery that needs to happen has to happen through only you. "

"Wow, you're a lot of help," I mumbled angrily and strolled quicker through the rock and rubble.

"I imagine you're hungry?" He called after me, and I stopped. My stomach was grumbling from hunger and had been for a while, despite my desire to ignore him and be angry. I guessed that he wouldn't eat, or couldn't eat, but that didn't have to stop me from attending to my own needs.

"Are you hungry?" I turned around and looked at him. He gave me a smile.

"Thought that would grab your attention," he smirked. "Can I interest you in some Baklava?"

Just the sound of the dessert made my stomach grumble louder, and the glint in his eye meant he had heard it. He extended his hand out toward me, and I felt my feet walk towards him, and my hand was in his. I remembered a time in health class when we learned about a case called "Stockholm Syndrome," and I knew the moment I grabbed his hand to go have dessert, I was under his spell for good.

Chapter Ten

The only sounds in our dark room were coming from next door. It sounded like whoever was in the next room was having an argument. The sounds from their TV were loud, and I was pretty sure someone was slamming their bathroom door. I was lying still in our bed. He was sitting in the white chair in the corner again. I waited to hear him breathe, sigh, snore, anything, but he didn't make a sound. I let out a soft sigh, hoping he wouldn't be awake to hear it. I wanted nothing more than for him to be asleep. I heard the movement of his head as he turned to look at me in the dark. I wondered if he could see me, instead of the still shadow that I could only make of him. We hadn't spoken a word to each other after dinner. Only soft sighs that came from me. He might have grunted once when we watched Greek television. Maybe.

Dinner had been different. Nothing like what I was used to with my family. High dining was something that he relished in while in Athens. He drove us to a restaurant called "Varoulko" where they served us soup, and sea bass, and all kinds of things that I hadn't been used to. I suddenly missed my mother's TV-dinners and wished we were back in the United States. I could hear my mother's voice throughout dinner repeating, "I need my grease."

"You're very quiet tonight. Is there anything on your mind?" he asked me as he picked at his plate.

"I'm just thinking about my mother," I said with a slight smile. "I miss the TV-dinners."

"This isn't to your liking?" He glanced at my full plate, and I gave him a small shrug.

"You're talking to an American. We like our cheeseburgers and fries," I smirked. He laughed and gave a nod.

"I'll have to remember that for the next meal." He lifted his fork up to his lips, and I watched intently. Was he really eating, or was he just pretending? Did Gods really eat food?

"Do you eat? Like, are you really eating that?" I asked, gesturing to his plate. He gave me a confused look for a moment and then down at his plate.

"Why wouldn't I eat? I am human."

"So, you have to eat when you're in your human form?"

He stared at me for a moment, looking as if he were debating what he should say. What wouldn't shock me? "Let's just say, when I'm like this, yes. I have to eat." He picked at his fish and brought more to his lips.

"Do you have a favorite or anything?" I asked with eagerness. I felt like this was the first time that I was getting inside of his mind.

He shook his head and lifted more fish to his mouth, and chewed it silently.

"Really? Nothing that you really prefer the best?"

"Food is nourishment to me. I don't care what it is."

"So, if someone gave you the grossest thing in the world to eat, you'd eat it?" I asked with a smile. He chuckled as he set his fork down on the table.

"Let me put it this way. For me— for us— the Gods," he directed his hand toward the sky, "Food isn't necessary for us. It's more of a way for us to blend into the crowd of humans. It's enjoyable, no doubt when the food is prepared well. So if someone offered me the grossest thing in the world, as you put it, I wouldn't be bothered to eat it."

"But you have a human's body, don't you? Don't you have to treat yourself the same way, we—humans—do?"

"Do I?"

"I can touch you, and you feel human," I said, reaching for his hand. He stared at our fingers as they touched for a moment. I felt a shock run through my skin again, as it had before, and I watched as he pulled his hand away.

"I'm as human as you want me to be, Summer. I'll be as human as I can be for you," he whispered, and I believed him. I felt as if he was trying to say much more to me, and my cheeks burned slightly from embarrassment. He was the first one to look away and glance back at his plate. It seemed that he debated if he really wanted to continue on with the charade, but after a moment, he lifted his fork and began to eat again. We ate quietly, the only sound coming from the clanking of our silverware hitting the pure, white plates. I mostly picked at my dinner. Our waiter brought out a beautiful dessert, one that I almost didn't want to touch at first.

"What is that?" I asked, breaking the silence as I looked at the purple-pink glob that was decorated with little elaborate flowers and fruit that was placed in front of me.

The waiter smiled at me and tried to say in the best English possible, "Pomegranate Panna Cotta."

"Isn't that Italian or something?" I glanced up at the waiter, but he shrugged and went over to the other tables that were waiting for his attention. I glanced at Hades, who continued to eye me as he lifted a seed to his mouth.

"You don't really think that I'm going to eat this, do you? When it's coming from you?"

He stared at me and then at my plate.

"I didn't make the dessert, Summer." He knew exactly what I was talking about. I wasn't stupid. Just as he had said earlier, when we first met, I knew the story. I knew the trick. I knew about the seeds.

"I know what these seeds mean to you," I said as I pushed my plate toward him. He bit his bottom lip with frustration. It was all over his face. A part of him hoped I'd eat a seed. Even if it was merely a seed, it meant something much more to him. It was years of my life, her life, that would be owed.

"You could, at least, try it, Summer."

"I'm not going to fall into any trap set by you," I said as I gave him a dirty glare.

"It's not a trap. It's dessert."

"Is that what you told *her* too?" I snapped as I leaned back in my chair and crossed my arms. He gently put his fork down beside his dessert plate and leaned across the table toward me.

"Please don't make a scene here, Summer. It's just dessert. I don't have control over everything as you think I might."

"How can I trust you?" I wanted to go back to the hotel room. I was done playing his stupid mind games. I wanted to go back home. Back to Point Judith. I wanted to go back to school and be an art student. I wanted it to be just like before I met him. I wanted my parents.

"Have I ever given you a reason to not trust me?" he asked with a genuine look of concern. I looked down at the untouched dessert and didn't speak until the waiter came back.

"Is there something wrong with your dessert?"

I didn't make the effort to reply back to the waiter. I heard *him* reply back instead.

"Μπορείτε να πάρετε ακριβώς μακριά. Αυτή δεν πεινάει "he mumbled towards the waiter. When I gave him a curious look, he frowned. "I told him to take it away, that you weren't hungry." The plate was lifted away, and the check was left in its place.

"I'm sorry about dinner," I murmured, glancing at his shadow as he sat in the white chair. He didn't make a sound. I knew I deserved it. I deserved every ounce of his silence. I slowly sat up and pulled the covers away, exposing my skin to the cool air. It felt refreshing to escape the heated covers.

"Are you asleep?"

"No," he replied with a hard voice. That should have been a sign for me to leave him alone. It should have been a sign for me to go back under the covers and try to sleep, but it wasn't. I walked around the bed and sat on the corner closest to him.

"I'm sorry," I whispered, trying again, reaching out in the dark, hoping that I would find a piece of him that I could grab. I felt bad.

"Go back to bed, Summer." His tone was harsh, but it didn't scare me enough to listen to him. Instead, I stood up and walked closer to his chair, until I bumped into his legs. The darkness was easier to see in now with the help of the slightly bright spotlight outside, peeking through the adjustable blinds; his image was easier to make out. He was silent and still. I reached out and touched his hair, letting my fingers trail through until they reached his shoulders. I heard him take a deep breath, and he touched my hand with his.

"What are you doing?"

"Trusting you," I whispered and felt his fingers intertwine with mine. It felt right. It felt so odd to feel so right with this stranger. That's what he was to me, no matter how much I wanted to believe that I knew him. I realized then, that I only knew *of* him, but not *who* he really was. I felt his arm wrap around my waist and pulled me closer toward him. My own heart was racing. I had never been around men much. College boys just weren't an interest of mine. Even in high school, I was too preoccupied with grades and art to pay too much notice to them. But there was no avoiding Hades. There was no avoiding his feelings toward me, or mine toward him. I had always loved him. I always loved the idea that I created of him. But even now, he was more alive than he had been in my dreams. He was more human than I ever imagined a God could be. He was real. He was right in front of me, and he was all I had left.

I heard him take a deep breath, placing his cheek against my stomach. My hands searched his soft hair, feeling the warmth and softness.

"Do you sleep too?" I whispered, wondering how childish I sounded.

"Yes, I sleep. When I can," his voice was smooth and soothing.

"You can't be comfortable sitting here." There was a silence in the room that not even I wanted to break. I wondered if he knew that I wanted his presence near me. I longed for it. He was all I had; he was all I wanted now. I could hear him suck in a breath; I knew then he understood my message hidden in my words.

"Go back to bed, Summer," he said, pushing me away from him slowly. I noticed his eyes were on me, scanning my face and our touching limbs. He wanted me the way I wanted him. Perhaps he understood it better than I did. Maybe he'd say that I wasn't ready yet. I still had all this "discovering" to do. A small ball of anger in my stomach started to twist and grow.

"I can't," I said, shaking my head. "I can't sleep."

"Try counting sheep or something. Apparently it's supposed to help," he said, pushing me away again, as I tried to fight back. I grabbed the arms of the chair and glared at him. I wasn't even sure if he could see my facial expression, but I didn't want him to push me away.

I wanted him to let me stay. I didn't want to go back to the cold bed and feel bad for dinner again. I didn't want to think about my dead parents. I didn't want to think about the darkness in the room, and how he was the darkest part. I just wanted the comfort that I had at the beach. I wanted home. I wanted home so desperately. I almost felt like I had forgotten about my life before this. My paints, my dreams, and my world I had created. His hands released me, and he gently shoved me toward the bed to face my fears, alone.

"I wish I could paint," I whispered, feeling the longing take over me. I missed my colors, my palettes, and my paper; the soothing feeling that I got from painting.

He remained still and silent in his chair, and I knew to give up. I knew to just go to bed, press my body into the sheets and wait for the sun to rise. I wonder what would happen then. Would he finally turn to me and tell me it was time to go? The fear of not knowing what was waiting for me filled me with pain in my chest that I almost wanted to let out with tears. There were invisible chains around my wrists, and no one could free me, not even myself. I followed the coverlet back to the front of the bed and climbed in, hoping that I would fall asleep fast. I knew that nothing would be alright in the morning. My bonds would still be there, and he would still be in the same chair.

* * * *

"Are you awake?" His voice was soft, and I felt a hand soothe my hair back over my ear. I pushed the pillow beside me over my face and violently shook my head.

"It cannot be time to get up, go away," I groaned sleepily as I lifted my arm over the pillow, to keep it in place. I felt the bed shift, and then the pillow was gone, and I was sitting upright in the bed.

"If we're going to where I want to take you, we have to get up now. We can't be seen."

"What? Where are we going?"

"Just get up, Summer. I can't tell you just yet," he said soothingly, as I felt his hands in my hair again, this time brushing my bangs out of my face. I slowly opened my eyes and saw the room was slightly dark; the sun wasn't completely up yet.

"Oh my god. What time is it?" I asked, angry that I was awake so early. Angry that I hadn't gone to bed earlier when he had told me to.

"It's a little after five. I'm giving you fifteen minutes. Go," he said, pointing to the bathroom door. I pulled myself out of bed slowly. I felt like an old woman with my arms and back aching; my head was swimming with the lack of sleep, and I was sure that the trembling I felt would stay with me for the day. As I entered the white bathroom, I noticed clean clothes were already laid out for me. They didn't even look like they belonged to me. What happened to my stretched out jeans and large t-shirts? These were clingy and more girly than I was used to. The shirt was white and soft to the touch, with soft beading around the neckline, while the jeans were freshly pressed and looked as if they'd be a second layer of skin rather than clothing. They seemed to appear from a magazine ad, designed for a model or a great beauty: neither was I.

"I want my real clothes," I demanded, opening the door into the dark room.

"Those are real clothes," He replied. "They have buttons and everything." He was a smartass.

"No, these aren't mine. I want my clothes I packed for Greece."

"I picked some things up on the way to the hospital the other day. Don't you like them?"

"They're a nice thought, but today, I want my clothes."

I heard a rustle of movement and then he was standing in the doorway, holding up one of my tie-dye shirts. "This is what you want?"

"Yes," I whispered, grabbing the shirt from his hands. I suddenly felt childish, choosing something so plain and ugly compared to what he had left for me.

"Why isn't that shirt to your liking?" he asked as he pushed the door open and pointed to the shirt on the sink counter.

"It's just… not me…" I drifted and lowered my eyes to my shirt in my hands.

"You're my…" he stopped and shook his head. "Never mind. Wear what you want. I was just trying to do something nice for you."

"And I thank you for the thought," I began. "I just want some normalcy."

"You're never going to know that normal again, Summer. You have to make a new normal for yourself."

"And I will, but it doesn't have to be on your terms," I stated.

He nodded and lifted his hands in surrender. "Touché. I'll leave you to get dressed." He closed the door before I could get another word in, not that I knew what I'd say to him. I just hoped that whatever he had planned was worth waking up at five for.

The sky was dark, and the sun was only a sliver in the sky. There was hardly anyone out on the sidewalks or streets. Athens was still asleep. Why weren't we?

"Where are we going?" I asked, almost afraid of the answer. I wasn't ready to hear him say, 'below.' I prayed for any answer but that one.

"You'll see," he murmured softly as he turned onto another road. There were twists and turns and tall buildings that were offices, stores, and apartments. All of the buildings looked ancient in their own way, full of history and stories. I wondered who lived in them. The car suddenly came to a slow stop, and he turned off the ignition.

"Can you tell me now?" I asked, looking around the alley that he had parked us in.

"Your parents never got to show you this place," he said slowly. That was my hint, and that's all he had to say to me. I knew what he was saying. I knew what this place was. This would have been my home. I looked at him for a moment, full of confusion and sadness.

"Why are we here?"

"To get the rest of your things. Whatever else you want. The Athens Police and such will be coming for the rest soon, and will probably dispose of whatever is left. Send it back to America, to your other family."

"And I had to come in the dead of the morning…?"

"Because I didn't want them to see you," he stated, probably not wanting to be questioned, but I wanted more than just that answer.

"Why didn't you want me to be seen?"

"You'd be taken away, Summer," he said, pushing his door open. "And I wouldn't be able to do anything about it. As long as you're with me, you're safe. Please do this my way."

"We do everything your way," I grumbled under my breath as I got out of the car and gently shut the door. "How am I not safe away from you?"

"Let's think about that one, now shall we? Where would you be without me?"

"I might be poor, and homeless, but I wouldn't be in danger."

"Oh really? Should I leave you for the Greek men then?"

"No!" I squealed, grabbing onto his arm. He lifted his finger up to his lips. I nodded and let go of him, distancing myself away from him. I glanced at the cobblestone road, looking at the tan buildings made of rock and brick. It was a scene almost from a postcard, resembling the many my father had sent to me while his stay in Greece, coming to life in front of me. It was no longer a photo to hang up on a wall, but a place that I could stand in front of, and touch.

"Do you want your paints? Your paintings?" He asked, grabbing my hand and pulling me into a doorway.

"I can have them?" I whispered in shock.

"Why couldn't you have them? You can have whatever you desire." I knew he could make anything happen. He was Hades, but I also knew that I would be limited to what I could take with me. I knew that I couldn't fit all my paintings in the hotel room, nor could I bring them to the place he was going to eventually take me. Those paintings that were boxed up in the place where my father and mother were going to make their home belonged to another girl. Another Summer. Not me. That Summer died with her parents.

He opened the door to where I would have been living, and inside were mountains of boxes. Some were opened, but most weren't. The ones with my name were piled in the narrow hallway. My father must have picked them up, but didn't want to do anything with them until my mother and I arrived. He was the kind of person that liked to do things as a family, even something as mundane as unpacking. I watched as Hades started to pick up boxes that had "Kitchen" and "Bedroom," moving them out of the way so that he could access the boxes that were mine. He was ready to take what I wanted and leave, quickly. I knew why he was so afraid. He had me now. And he didn't want anyone to change that.

"Do you remember which boxes you put your paints in?"

"I put my paints together in one box with all my brushes and my leftover paper."

"All in one?" he asked, surprised.

"Yes, all in one. Why?"

"Well, that came in handy. I just have to carry one box," he said with a smile and started to rip the tops of the boxes open until he came across my painting box. I couldn't tear my eyes away from the off-white walls. Everything was cream and peach. Everything had my mother written all over it. My dad had already begun to decorate the house with pictures of us. Pictures of temples, and rocks, and fossils.

"Do you want anything else from here?" He startled me, and I glanced over at his work of the boxes.

"Why are you in such a hurry? No one knows we're here."

"I just don't want to cause a scene."

"As if you couldn't avoid that," I said, shaking my head. "Give me the real reason."

"I am," he stated. His tone told me to stop questioning and get on with my picking and choosing.

"Am I allowed to take more?" I asked, glancing around the room again.

"How much more do you want?" he asked as he raised his eyebrows in bemusement.

"I want something to remember my parents by," I murmured, bending over one of the boxes he tore apart by accident. My mother's handwriting was on the side that said: 'Bedroom.' My mother's jewelry case was gently squeezed between sheets and pillowcases. It was like her to keep her most expensive things in the places that no one would think they'd be in. I lifted the small wooden container out of the cardboard box and gently opened the lid. My mother's gold necklace and matching earrings were scattered among the rest of her other belongings in it, including my father's class ring.

"I'm going to keep this," I said as I glanced up at his soft face. He gave me a curt nod and glanced around the room. "Anything else you want?" I shook my head, glancing around at the other boxes. They were just things. All replaceable. Just as I would be to the world.

"Then, let's go," he murmured, grabbing my belongings with his arms. I followed closely behind, giving one last glance back at the house where I would have lived; where I would have made a life until *he* came for me.

Chapter Eleven

"Can I ask you a question?" I whispered, glancing up at the dark ceiling. I could see the hint of the red alarm clock numbers reflecting in the corner of the room, and I wondered what time it was. I knew it was well past one a.m.

"You're still awake?" He replied sounding annoyed.

"What did you mean at dinner the other night?" I continued on, ignoring his comment and the tone of his voice.

"What are you talking about?" He snapped. I could tell he wanted me to sleep already, but I wasn't ready to. I wanted answers; I was tired of sleeping in the dark with the mysterious stranger that I wanted to know. I knew him only as Hades, but I didn't know his desires. His thoughts.

"The part when you told me you'd try to be human enough for me," I whispered. I heard him suck in a breath. "What do you think it takes to be human?"

"Summer, I really don't want to talk about this."

"But I do. We always do things your way. If I'm going to be stuck with you for the rest of my life, I'm going to expect some boundaries to be crossed."

"Oh, are you?" he asked amused. I could hear him shift in his chair, and I slowly sat up, pushing the coverlet off of my body.

"I want answers. I deserve them."

"Well, I don't know about that," he said with a small laugh. His small laugh drug me out of bed, to where he was sitting.

"Please?" I could already feel the tears spring to life. I knew that he couldn't see them there in the darkness of the room, and I didn't want him to. I put my hands on my cheeks, wanting the burning sensation to go away.

"It's not that I won't tell you things."

"Then, why do you treat me like this? You don't give me a name to call you. You don't answer my questions. You tell me things that I don't understand and tell me that I'll understand later. I can't wait for later. I need to know things now."

"You think you need to know now, but you don't."

"Stop! See? You're doing it again."

"Summer, this is only the beginning. The journey with me is far from over," he said. I could hear the promise in his voice. I knew there was more. I knew that there was something more for me; I just didn't understand it yet. I knew that there was still the journey to the underworld waiting for me— the gods and the souls. The stories that I thought were all just pretend.

"When are you going to take me down to your world? You took me. You have me. What are you waiting for?"

"I was waiting for you to recover," he whispered. I heard him shift again in the chair and this time, I felt his hand on my wrist. His thumb was making light circles over my veins.

"You're almost healed completely, and that's good. If I had taken you down to my world, the way you were with your injuries, you wouldn't have stood the chance of survival. Where I live, death dominates. You would have died."

"And you wouldn't have been able to do anything?"

"I'm only the ruler. I'm to protect the dead, not determine who lives or dies. The Fates decide that."

"Why do you scare me?" I whispered after a long moment of silence. In his eyes, I saw the truth and saw the journey that he spoke of. There was much to be afraid of. I hadn't meant to say it aloud, but it came out all the same. I saw his face more clearly, then. It was much closer than before. "I'm so scared, that I'm so drawn to you. I can't help but want to be around you."

"Yes…" he whispered. I felt his hands pull on both of my arms, lowering me to my knees. I was tucked in between his strong legs. He was warm and much more than just a dark shadow. He was a dark Prince.

"Why have you done this to me?" I heard my voice shake, and tears started to fall down my cheeks.

"You haven't guessed already?" he asked with concern. I felt his hands on my face, and his breath was on my lips. His fingers were cool and rough, yet soft and warm, gentle and familiar. I wanted him to never stop touching me, and the thought scared me. I had no control over my thoughts or my body. I felt my hands creep up onto his shoulders; my fingers twisted themselves into his long, black hair.

"Just tell me. Please tell me," I begged. I needed to hear it. I needed to be sure that I wasn't dreaming. He wasn't a dream, and this wasn't just a dream world that I was living in.

"Summer, the pomegranates? The paintings you drew of me? You're drawn to me; I mean, look around you! You're in Greece! You're in the very setting of your own Greek story!"

"I know, I know!" Tears began to pour onto his fingers, and I tried to wipe them away. As I did, I felt him tip my chin up toward his face. I wanted this. I wanted this so badly. I wanted his lips on mine. I had dreamt about it, even before he had been real in front of me. My breath was asking to be kissed, and a moment later his lips crushed against mine. It was real. His hands were in my hair, and mine were tousled in his. He smelled like the beach, my beach, and it brought more tears to my eyes. He was my beach, my home, and my life. He was breathing air into me, giving me the will to do the unthinkable with him— to go beyond my human world, and enter his immortal one. He smelled like the waves and the earth. A mixture of everything. I wanted to be consumed by him, live underneath his soft skin and exist through the crust of my old paints. He gently pushed me back, watching me as I struggled to keep my eyes open.

"I don't know how to make it any clearer to you." His eyes were wide and serious, and I knew all the answers were in the kiss. I knew what he was trying to say. I knew what I needed to know. I just didn't want to accept it. How could this be happening to me? Me, of all the people in the world, of all the girls who existed, he picked me. My lips felt empty and cold without his there. Now that I had a taste of him, I wanted more. I wanted to grab his shoulders and press his lips against mine again and take the heat and the life he offered.

"Do you need to sit on the bed?"

"Yes," I murmured quickly, pushing his chest away, trying to regain my mind, my balance, and my pulse as I sat on the coverlet. I felt the kiss flow through my body, sending shivers down my spine. The kiss has shaken me; caused me to feel as if I were falling into tiny pieces that would fit so perfectly in his hand. Did he know he was my first kiss? I felt his hand grab my wrist, and he gently pushed me down onto the bed. I didn't know what to say, and I waited for him to speak, but he reflected the same silence.

"Why did you do that?" I whispered shakily, touching my lips with my fingertips and glanced at him. He stood silently in front of me. I could feel his dark gaze burning into my skin. I knew that whatever answer he was going to give me wouldn't be the truth or the answer that I wanted to hear.

"I think you should go to bed now, Summer," he whispered softly.

"No. This time, I'm going to stay here and wait for answers," I demanded, digging my fingers into the comforter. I wanted it to be a statement, but I knew that if he picked me up, I had no chance of winning the fight. I wanted to know why he kissed me. I wanted to know if his kiss meant the same to him as it did to me.

"I don't know what to tell you."

"You know everything," I snapped. "You can't play that card, anymore!"

"I can play whatever card I want," he bit back at me.

"Why did you kiss me?" My tone was harsh and upset. The dizziness of his lips was wearing off, and I was touching reality again.

"Did you not want me to? Because I thought you wanted me to," he asked, raising his eyebrow, seeming to think that I would just give in to his answer. He wanted to hear me say 'yes.' I wouldn't give him the satisfaction.

"You know what, I will go to bed. Have a nice night in your chair." I stood up, shoving him out of the way the best I could, and reached for the tossed blankets.

"Oh, no you don't," he grumbled, grabbing my arm and pulling me back against him as if I were a doll. He wasn't finished talking to me.

"I don't understand what you want from me!" I shouted, transforming us into the couples that surrounded our rooms; their loud voices in the night, the TV channels, the showers, the tears. We were just another noisy room now. I tried to pry myself out of his arms, but he didn't let go of me. He could have been afraid that I would run out of the door, but I knew that I wouldn't be able to get far, and I knew he'd find me. I had nowhere to go.

"You want to know what I want from you?" he grunted as I struggled more. I could feel my wrists burn under his touch; I knew I'd have bruises in the morning.

"Let go of me," I shouted louder. I wanted the world to hear me. I willed someone to come in and save me. I had to believe that my father or my mother would come in and take me away. I felt his lips touch my neck, and a sizzle of tingles jolted down my arm, causing my body to relax. I should have resisted; I didn't want him to win.

"I want you to remember, Persephone. I want you to remember what happened to you, what happened to us. Remember me. Remember my love for you. Remember your love for me. Remember what your mother did to you. Remember how you felt. I need you to remember what happened...."

"Stop calling me Persephone!"

"Remember what it was like when I first took you. Remember when I kissed you. Remember your sorrow and your joy, the way she made you feel, the way I made you feel. Remember." I shoved my hands against his chest, pulling my body away from him. There was nothing to remember. My mind was blank. There was nothing but distant shadows that I didn't understand. Picture stills of faces that I didn't know, and events that I didn't comprehend.

"Let go of me!"

"Please remember!"

"There's nothing to remember. Absolutely nothing!" I shouted. It was almost a scream. I knew someone had to have heard me by now. There had to be help coming for me. This was too nice of a hotel for listeners to ignore it.

"Lies! Why are you fighting it? Why are you fighting her, Summer? Let her blossom. She was meant to blossom. Let her live in you again!" he shouted at me. I felt his words flow through me like the blood in my veins. She was alive. Something was alive in me. But I didn't want her to win.

"She's not me! I'm Summer, not a figment of your imagination!"

"She's real too, Summer. She's there in your memory. She exists. She's just waiting for you to remember her." I shoved harder against him. He held onto me so tightly that I was afraid if I fought anymore, my limbs would give way, and fall off. They were so weak and so tired already from pushing against him.

"Please let go of me!" I screamed. This time, I had his attention. I felt his grip let go, and I fell against the bed.

"You're insane. I knew from the very beginning you were," I began; fresh tears were flowing down my face. "Stay away from me!" I jolted my body up and reached for the nearby wall. My fingers guided me toward the closest door. Space and distance could only be the cure for now.

"It's time for us to go," he stated firmly. I saw him closing in on me, and I raced to the door. I didn't even care that I didn't have shoes on. I was going to run. I was going to get help. I needed to let go of this stranger and go home. I needed to go home to my beach, even though I knew that I could never return there. He'd find me there too. Would my life now always be something I'd have to live on the run? I swung the door open and ran. I didn't care where my feet took me.

"Where do you think you're going?" he shouted after me. I didn't care where I was going, didn't he understand that? I just knew I had to get away. The white carpet led me to the choice of the elevator or the stairs. The stairs were clearly my best option.

"You're not going to escape me, Summer," his voice echoed in the stairwell. I could hear his shoes on the steps, and they sounded so close. I didn't stand a chance, but I knew I had to make the attempt.

"Leave me alone. Please leave me alone," I heard myself sob. I was panicking. I held onto the stairwell banister as hard as I could with every turn. I felt like I would fall at any moment.

"I really don't want to do this, Summer. Please don't make me do things that make you unhappy."

So many thoughts raced through my mind as his voice echoed down the stairwell. If he didn't want to make me unhappy, why was he so hell-bent on keeping me where I didn't want to be? Why did he take me away from my home? Why were my parents dead?

"Stop! Please," I begged. I couldn't even see anymore. My tears blurred the path. My feet missed a step, and I tumbled to another landing. I felt pangs of pain flow through my arms and legs, but I pushed myself up. I saw the blur of a door and hoped it would be the source of my freedom. I reached for the door and began to pull on the knob as hard as I could. It was locked. I was stuck. There was only one more floor left, and I knew in my heart that door would be locked too. I sunk to the floor, my body in a miserable ache. My face felt hot and wet from sweat and tears.

"Are you ready to stop running?" he asked as he stood in front of me.

I sobbed harder, creating quakes in my body that I couldn't control. I knew that I was his prey. I had nowhere else to run. I tried and failed. I should have known better.

"Will you go back upstairs with me?" he asked as my sobs became quieter. I wiped my hand across my eyes but didn't dare to look up at him. I still had the desire to run. I wanted to test my leg, but I knew his strong hands would grab me and pull me back. He'd pull me down into his darkness, and I'd drown in it.

"Did you hurt yourself?" he asked as he bent down to touch me.

"Don't you touch me," I snapped, glaring at his soft face, slapping his hand away from me. It was full of remorse. Not at all what I had expected to see, but my anger prevented me from caring.

"Let me help you," he whispered, gathering me into his arms and began to carry me back up the stairwell. There was no one in the hallway. There weren't any voices. I wondered if anyone even bothered to consider helping me. Had they hidden away in their bathrooms, hoping that I would be the only victim?

As we entered our room, he gently let me down onto my feet and turned to lock the door. I knew I had terminated the trust between us. He was afraid I'd run again and again. I pulled myself into the cold bed and tugged the covers over my head. I imagined one of my blank canvases and the colors that I would use if I could. The splatter of hot red anger mixed in with the sad tones of blue and purple. He wanted me to let her blossom within me, and I would. I'd let her blossom into the lonely person that I was. I'd paint him a flower that had wilted and died— black and fever purple with dead, blue veins. This is what had become of his Persephone.

"There is your Persephone." She's dead.

Chapter Twelve

"It's time to wake up." His voice shook me awake, and I was up before his hands could find me. His face looked tired and strained, and I wondered if he had struggled to sleep. Had I finally won at a battle? He and I packed everything that we could and together, brought it down to the car. I knew what this meant: This was it. These were my last moments in my world. These were my last moments of being just Summer. Though I knew after last night; I would never be just Summer again. I never had been just me; *she* had always been a part of me without me ever knowing.

He drove us over the Greece countryside. Four hours' worth of silence. One tree became hundreds of other trees. One road led to others, and as the day began to awaken and the sun began to shine a little brighter and warmer, I rolled down the window on my side and let the air wash over my skin. I knew to enjoy it before it was all gone forever. I smelled the ocean before I even saw it.

"Where are we going?" I was the first to break the silence, and I studied his face for a moment. He looked confused and torn, yet determined. His jaw was tense.

"Have you ever heard of 'the Gates of Hades'?"

My chest tightened. Of course, I knew about it. It was located in Cape Matapan, the most southern point of Greece. It was there that Spartans had built Poseidon, the God of the Seas, a temple. It is also said that when Hercules went to find the entrance to Hades to fulfill his last labor, it was there in Cape Matapan that he found the entrance. My parents had told me about it once when I asked about a temple for Hades. According to other traditions and stories, Hades and Persephone had a temple of their own called, "Necromanteion," but the true location was debated between scholars and archeologists.

"Yes, I have," I murmured. "Is that where we're going?"

"We're going to stay in town overnight. In the morning, we'll head the rest of the way."

"What town are we staying in?" I looked back out the window, trying to catch the name of where we were.

"Gythion. It's a nice little town near the ocean," he murmured softly.

"I've never heard of it."

"Well, now you'll never forget it," he said with a sigh as he adjusted one of the knobs on the dash. "It's a really great place." A blast of cooler air blew against my cheeks, and I pushed one of the air vents closed.

"Been there often?" I retorted.

"Not often enough, I'm afraid," he smirked as he adjusted one of the vents to blow on himself and quickly dashed a look at me. I wasn't sure if he was serious or not. I decided to not ask and turned my face to look out the window. The scenery was all the same; the clouds were white, the sky was a beautiful sea-blue. The kind of blue that most people wished they could see. And the call of the ocean was always right around the corner. The faster he drove, the closer I knew we were getting to the town, and to the gates that would lead me to a completely different world. The rest of the drive was long, and when we finally arrived in Gythion, I was exhausted. We still had the rest of the afternoon to get through. I wondered if I could manage an escape; if it would be as disastrous as the night before. The thought of it sent shivers down my spine. The impact of falling, my twisting limbs echoed like a bad dream in my mind. My mind wanted to get away, but my heart knew there wouldn't ever be a successful chance. He pulled up to a building that slightly reminded me of the hotel in "Pretty Woman." It was a five-story whitewashed hotel. The last three top stories were balconies to the rooms it encased. Over the front doors were the words, "Hotel Nanoen," but on a nearby canopy, the words "Hotel Gythion" greeted us. It looked nice and public.

"I'll check us into a hotel, and from there, we can go sightseeing if you want."

"I'm not really in the mood to sightsee," I mumbled, taking in my surroundings. The ocean was on my side of the car. I wanted so desperately to sink my toes into the sand. I wanted to dig up my paints and leave a part of myself for the mortal world, so they'd know I had been here.

"Then I'll just go and check us in, and we can hang out in the room." I didn't give him a reply. My eyes were too transfixed on the ocean. It made me long for my beach home, my sand, my waves, my room, and my parents. It was different in the sense that my beach was mine. There hadn't been advertising, umbrellas, or nudists. It had just been me and my paints and the few joggers in the morning and night. It seemed like the matter of minutes that he was back and was grabbing our luggage from the back of the car. He didn't say a word, just motioned for me to follow him in, which I did. The lobby was warm with brown chairs and gray tiles. I followed him up a few flights of stairs to the third floor, where he opened a small door and led me into a room that I wasn't expecting. The room was a soft yellow, warm and inviting, and I could feel the very calming ocean breeze blowing throughout the room. As I limped farther into the room, the bed stuck out to me the most. I certainly hoped he had the same plan as in the other hotel. I had no intentions of sharing the bed with him. Ever--Actually.

"There is a sofa in the sitting room. I'm going to sleep there," he said, almost as if he were reading my mind.

"Yeah, you should be used to sleeping in chairs," I said, glancing at him as he walked toward the large windows, pushing the curtains away to expose the large doors that led to one of the balconies I saw from the outside.

"Thanks for the invitation," he said sarcastically, turning toward me with a smirk. I returned it with a glare.

I put my bag on the floor and dug through the box that he had put on the table, near the bed. My paints were still fresh and usable. I knew exactly what I wanted to do. "Are we allowed to go out on the deck?"

"I paid for it. I don't see why you can't," he said with a shrug. "You can do whatever you want."

"I can do whatever I want?" I asked, giving him a glare. Of course, now he would say I could do what I wanted. I was free to roam around, as long as I stayed in the designated places that he decided upon.

"How quickly you change your mind," I mumbled and grabbed my painting box. I watched his facial expressions turn into an annoyance.

I hadn't done this in so long. It felt like months. What day was it anyway? Monday? Wednesday? How long ago had my parents died? Time seemed to not exist with him. Time didn't have meaning anymore. I should have felt sad. I was alone in the world. I seemed to almost forget that my parents were dead. The world and I had moved on so fast. I didn't really get the chance to mourn them. I glanced at my arm, noticing the slight bruise on my wrist from the other night. From the hold, he had on me. My bruises and cuts from the accident were almost gone completely. Soon, there wouldn't be a trace left of what happened to me. My parents' names would be traceless, as would I. They'd be buried underground, and I would be living there.

"I'll be outside," I stated matter-of-factly, and slid open the balcony door, letting the ocean wind hit my face. It tasted wonderful. It smelled even better than I remembered. I set my paints and my paper on the patio table and looked out over the road, toward the ocean and watched it, completely mesmerized. It was an understatement to call Gythion beautiful. It was a vast town of blue rooftops and an ocean that one would only see in either paintings or magazines specifically for travel. It was a place I wish I could have spent more time in. I knew I had to paint that longing and remember this place.

My brush dropped into an ocean blue and began to draw lines that became a shore. Black, into a face. And pink, into a fruit that was left in the sand. I didn't know what I'd do with the painting, but as I painted, I didn't care. I could leave it as a gift for the cleaning lady, or tear it into pieces and toss it into the ocean water like I had before I had left home. I stayed out on the deck, enjoying the ocean breeze and the sound of cars as they passed by the hotel. It almost felt like I was home, except for knowing he was inside waiting. Always right behind me. I turned and gazed through the glass door, noticing that his still form was laid out on the white bed. I wondered if I could get away for a while, unnoticed. Would he sense that I wasn't on the deck anymore? He was a God, I was sure that eventually he'd find out, and he'd show up in the crowd and drag me back to the prison of the room and lock me away like one of the princesses in a fairy tale. Perhaps he was like Rothbart, from the story of "Swan Lake." He kidnapped the young Princess Odette and kept her for himself. Any attempt to leave ended disastrously for the young princess. The large, dark, looming form would forever haunt me; my fate would be the same as Odette. I knew there wasn't a prince in my destiny to save me. He was my destiny, and he, by no sense of the word, was a prince.

I tucked all my paints into a corner next to the door, sliding the bottles on top of the wet sheet of paper to hold it in place. I looked again, peering through the glass, checking for any movement from him. His chest expanded and diminished, gently. I wondered if he dreamt. And if he did, what was it he dreamt about? '*You already know he dreams about Persephone, you idiot,*' my mind repeated back to me. I didn't know why that thought disappointed me so much. I turned back to the deck rails and looked down at the road below. It wasn't that far down, and if it meant escaping for an hour or so, the climb was worth it.

I swung my legs over the railing and eased myself down as carefully as I could until the toe of my sneaker touched pavement. My legs couldn't carry me fast enough toward the ocean. The air carried a tangy smell of salt and water and suntan lotion. The familiar scent of paint was on my hands, and it was the closest that I would get to the smell of home. I very nearly almost smiled.

There were a few bodies littering the sand like rocks; men and women in skimpy bathing suits, and a few scattered children in the shallow waves with their yellow buckets and orange shovels. It was like watching one of my classmate's paintings come to life. A lot of them painted beach scenes with the typical child building a sand castle. The cool, salty breeze was liberating. As soon as I hit the sand, I slipped my shoes off and continued to walk toward the water until it licked over the tops of my feet. A tear escaped the corner of my eye and fell down my cheek.

What if I just ran away right now? What was stopping me? I could easily blend myself into the crowd of people. I could sleep on the beach. I could try to find a way back home to America. There had to be someone looking for me. I could find the American Embassy. They would know a way to get me back home. There had to be something that was left to me by my parents. I could survive. My heart churned as I watched the waves ebb and flow in front of me, almost as if they were beckoning me over the horizon. Something sank within my chest. I knew that I was tricking myself into a false hope. Even the feel of the ocean mocked me. I'd never go home. I'd never sit and paint near *my* ocean again. I glanced back at the hotel, fully knowing that I'd see his form on the balcony, watching me. Waiting to see if I'd run or not. He'd follow. He'd always follow. No matter where I went, he'd always be ten steps in front of me.

And sure enough, he was there, leaning out over the balcony. He was staring me down, and my heart jumpstarted into a panic. This was it. This was my chance. I had to take it. I ran.

The dry sand was hot on my feet as I raced up the beach toward the road. In my periphery, I saw him dash from the balcony. His instincts about me being a flight risk were correct, but I had to try one more time. I had to make sure that if I was given the opportunity to get away, that I used it to my full advantage.

I dashed up the street. I wanted to scream for help, but I knew that no one could help me. No one could tear me from the claws of Hades – from Death, himself. I was the only one who could keep myself from going under. More tears streamed down my face. The sound of his angered voice was in the wind. From behind me, he was calling my name. The frustration and the fury were evident in his voice, but it didn't stop me. I kept running. My bare feet hurt so badly, but I continued to race as fast as they could carry me. The pavement cut into my skin, and I knew that it would be hard to walk later. If there even *was* a later for me.

"Summer! Stop!" I heard him shouting behind me. People watched me run, pointing and mumbling to themselves in Greek. I wondered why they didn't help me. Glancing quickly behind me, I saw his dark form move faster and faster toward me. There was no way I'd out run him. I was already getting tired. My eyes fell to my feet, watching them hit the pavement; each step was more and more painful. Abruptly, a large hand grabbed hold of my arm and jolted me to stop. This stranger held me tightly in his grasp until Hades finally caught up with me. The air blazed in my chest, as I fought to catch my breath. I was done. Finished. Caught – like a wild animal.

"Is this who you want?" the man said, trying to form words in English underneath his thick, Greek accent. He had dirty blonde hair and hard, cold blue eyes. I fought as hard as I could to try to escape, but he pinned my wrists together with his large hand. I knew the shadow was there, his cold grasp on my upper arm.

"Thank you, sir."

"Did she steal?"

"No, nothing like that," he replied. I could feel him pulling me into his arms, and I knew my opportunity was over. I tried once and failed. I tried a second time and knew it would be the last. Hades tugged me along, turning away from the man and dragged me back in the direction of the hotel. I was sure my feet were bloody, wincing with the pain of each, disappointed step I took. I could feel eyes all around me. On me. Within me. I was stupid – so stupid to think for a second that I had the chance of escaping him. He was silent, grim, the entire way back.

When he shut the door behind us, locking me away again from the world, he sat me down on the chair and lifted my bare feet to take a look.

"You did something very stupid," he snapped, letting my feet fall onto the floor with a thud. I sucked in a sharp breath, the pain dashing up from my feet like jagged glass. I slumped over in the chair, focusing on my breathing.

"When are you going to learn?"

"When are you going to let me go? I just want to go *home*." I snapped, biting back the tears.

"You're not going home. You're coming with me."

"Can't you see that I don't want to?" I lifted my tear-soaked eyes to him, hearing the desperation fill my own voice.

"I don't care what you want, Summer," he shouted at me. He disappeared around the corner, into the bathroom. I heard the sound of drawers opening as he rustled around with papers of some kind. He came out with a roll of bandage and bent to begin wrapping it around my feet.

"Why is it so important that you keep me? What am I to you?" My voice broke in quiet sobs. I watched his face harden. His jaw tightened as he looked at me with that dark, cold look that sent shivers through my body.

"You are the carrier of Persephone's soul."

I blinked, silent for a moment, allowing that to sink in. "Is that all I am to you? A shell? A container which holds the person you really love?"

"Are you meant to be more, Summer?"

His biting words stabbed my heart, and I looked away from him. I wanted to pull my knees to my chest and curl into a ball, and just disappear. I lifted my hand to my eyes, wanting to shield the tears that were forming again in my eyes. I was just a device. Once Persephone was back and alive, he would do anything to push me away— to kill me off so she could live again. He didn't say anything to me. I felt his arms wrap around me and lift me up before he laid me gently on the bed.

"What if I don't want to remember her," I whispered, afraid of what he would say in return. The mattress gave against his weight, as he sat down next to me.

"It's not an option. You will."

Another tear began to roll, and I quickly wiped it away. I wasn't sure if I was crying from the pain in my feet, or the pain in my heart. He laid back so that we were side by side on the bed. I fought the urge to push him away. I wanted distance. I didn't want anything to do with him, but he shifted his body so that he was gazing down at me on the bed. My heart jumpstarted in my chest. His lips were so close to mine, and I couldn't stop watching them. The reminder of what had happened the night before was so fresh, so vivid in my head. His lips had been warm and soft against mine. My heart yearned for more, and I hated myself for it. He was my captor. I shouldn't want to kiss the man who was taking me away from my life and everything that I loved.

"You have to remember, Summer. If you don't, then you'll lose me forever."

"Good, then that'll solve everything," I snapped, turning my face away from his. The farther from his lips I was the better. However, I hated to admit that his words scared me for some reason. I didn't want to be without him forever, but I hated him. I wanted nothing to do with him, and yet, I knew from the beginning, that I couldn't live without him. He was real. My dark angel, my fantasy, was real.

"Where are you going?" he asked gently, a note of humor touching his words.

"I don't want you near me."

"You'll have to get used to that," he murmured softly, and I could almost hear the smile under his breath.

"I hate you."

"I hardly believe that," he said, pulling my body back toward him. I stared up into his black eyes, and I felt his fingers gently curl into my hair. His touch was like a spider's web.

"Believe it," I whispered. "I hate you."

"I think I'm very able to change your mind," he said with a teasing smile and began to lower his lips toward mine. I knew what was coming. My mind was screaming for me to turn my head. Reject him. Hurt him. But my heart wanted me to stay. My heart wanted his lips on mine again. They belonged there. I couldn't move. My eyes closed, and I was lost in the wave of color and touch. He was yellow. Pure yellow. The kind of yellow that was almost like honey, drizzling down over my spine, my arms, my wrist, my fingers— touching ever so gently. And then he began to deepen the kiss as if there was something he was trying to show me; prove to me. As if he had waited lifetimes to kiss my lips, her lips. . Our lips. I couldn't help but respond to him. My hands clenched his shoulders tightly, and he nipped at my lip; a small moan escaped from me before I had the chance to control it. Time seemed to speed around us. Night was approaching quickly. The cold would surround us and keep us captive in the bedcovers. I could imagine the painting, the style, and the colors; the black form, consuming the white form— the winter lord eating the spring maiden. I imagined the paint brushes coming to life on their own, forming pictures and scenes, figures and faces. His was the first. His pale face, his dark eyes, etching themselves into hers. In mine.

"You're my wife," he whispered to her. "I love you always." Her smile was sharp and pink. Her lips were like rose petals. I could almost smell the fragrance of summer on her skin. Her hair was long and golden. She was perfect. No wonder he loved her. I wanted to toss the dream away. I wanted him to love me, not her. I wanted him to love me for me, not because I was Persephone. I felt a tear fall down my cheek and mesh into both of our skins. Her love for him overwhelmed me, and I didn't know how to tell him.

"Yes, you see?" he said softly, bringing his hands through my hair. I wanted to cry. I wanted to tell him that I had seen too much. Too much for my little heart to handle. I turned my head to avoid his, and I felt his lips brush against my neck. He didn't say anything, only rolled over onto his back, letting out a heavy sigh and stared up at the ceiling.

"What happened to her?" I whispered finally, putting a stop to the silence between us. He glanced over at me and sighed again.

"Did Demeter do something to Persephone to keep her from you?"

"You know what Demeter did after I stole her daughter, don't you? She was so angry, so distraught that she forgot about the humans on the earth. She starved them. She had the power to kill off mankind. Zeus had to step in and force Persephone to go home with her mother. Persephone was so upset. I didn't know…" His voice drifted into silence as he picked at the white comforter.

"Is Demeter still alive?" I asked, already knowing the answer. Gods and Goddesses couldn't die. For some reason, Demeter had found the way to turn Persephone into me, a mortal. He looked at me and nodded his head.

"Very much alive."

"Then what… happened to Persephone? How did she become me?" I felt the tears of blue sadness fall down my cheeks again. There was no hiding them, this time. How could a mother's love push a woman to destroy the happiness of her child?

"I suppose we'll find that out together," he murmured. I stared at the ceiling for a few minutes, trying to picture the setting. What had happened to her? Why had she become me? How had a beautiful goddess become an imperfect, human painter? If Demeter was still alive and had something to do with keeping Persephone away from Hades, then what would happen to me? Did my family know who I was? Had they been trying to protect me from something I didn't understand?

'*Someone could kidnap you, and I'd never know.*' I could hear my mother's voice in my head repeating the same words she always did when I insisted on going out to the beach at night to paint. They annoyed me so much before, but now they made sense. My mind couldn't stop thinking, wondering, processing. It was full of colors and faces— things that were a blur, a distant memory that I wanted to grab. '*Please,*' I repeated over and over again. '*Please show me.*'

'*Drink this. Drink. Taste and drink,*' the words repeated over and over again. It wasn't my voice. It was just like the dream before. A cup, golden hair, a face. It was such a blur. I fought through the waves of time. '*Show me,*' I whispered in my mind. '*Show me the truth.*' The painting in our kitchen; Persephone and Demeter in a garden as Hades stood in the shadows of the forest. Demeter wanted her child to be free of his curse. Persephone wanted to be

127

free of her mother. Hades wanted to be loved. No one could win this game.

A narcissus flower; red and glorious among daisies and tiger lilies. The sun was high in the sky, and other maidens dressed in white and blue garments dashed through the tall grass. Their feet almost hovering as they jumped like elk through the valley. A hand, soft and smooth reached for the flower. Her golden hair touched her hand as she picked it and the earth erupted around her. His face, beautiful and dark meets hers, and his hand reaching out for her. She loved him the instant that she saw him, and he knew her all along. I squeezed my eyes tighter, fighting for the story to continue. I knew it by heart, but this was new. This was real. She hadn't been stolen. She wanted to go with him. There was no sun where he took her. The ocean was the bluest of blues, and the rocks were white, and then there was black. The air was stale and moist, and her heart thundered in her chest. A large river with floating orbs, a boat being pushed by a ghostly form. The dark ruler transformed from his human state to the dark king she knew him to be. Dark designs began to inch along his skin until he was completely covered. The designs were swirls and lines that made him seem mystical and mysterious.

"Can you love me like this?" he whispered into her golden hair and her laugh echoed throughout the dark hollows of the cave like bells. My stomach churned as her laugh echoed throughout my body. I hated her. The way she held him, the way she wasn't afraid of the dark, the way she was perfect.

"Drink this…" The voice appeared again, and the dark caves were gone. A woman stood silently, extending a cup

in her hand with an evil grin. The golden goddess took the
cup and began to drink the deep red liquid. I could feel it
falling past my lips. It was sweet and familiar.
Pomegranate. It was gone as soon as it had appeared. The
woman was gone, the taste was gone, and I was left with
nothing but the night. I felt hands on my shoulders, shaking
me back and forth. It was almost like I was under water,
and I couldn't catch my breath.

"Summer, wake up!" His voice was so close. I tried to
swim through the darkness, seeking fresh air, but the
shaking made it nearly impossible.

"Wake up, Summer…" he whispered

"Wake up Summer." Persephone smiled.

" Wake up." I gasped.

His voice. Her voice. My voice. My eyes flashed open
to his concerned face, and I felt his finger touch the bottom
of my eye, wiping the wetness away.

"It was just a dream," he whispered, holding me
against his chest.

Chapter Thirteen

"Are we there yet?" I whispered as I leaned my head against the car window. I heard Hades chuckle lowly, and he patted my knee with his free hand.

"I didn't know you were so anxious to get there."

"I'm not. I'm nervous," I said, letting out another deep yawn. I hadn't slept well at all past my dream last night. After the visions of Persephone and Hades together, I was haunted by her beauty and the woman with the cup. Was she Demeter? Was she a Goddess that worked for Demeter? Had she killed Persephone with her drink? I could still almost taste the sweet poison.

"What are you nervous about?" he asked, giving me a confused glance. I shrugged, tucking myself more against the car door.

"Am I going to die?" I voiced quietly. The thought had passed through my mind more than once.

"No, you're not going to die," he murmured.

"But I'm human. Won't my soul want to go to the afterlife or something?"

"You're not going to die," he repeated, letting out a sigh. "I promise."

There was no reason to ask him any more questions. I didn't want to scare myself with the thought that I was about to sink into the deepest cave in the world. I wanted to close my eyes and sleep, but I didn't want to be haunted by the faces that were lurking behind every blink that I made. I didn't want to see them anymore.

"We're almost there. You should get packed up," he said, motioning to my exposed iPod and book that were in my lap.

"I think I can just stuff these in my bag when we get out," I said, glancing up at him. "Unless you have plans of jumping from the car while it's still moving, and causing this huge, dramatic scene. In which case, you're right! I should really get myself together."

"Fine," he snapped and looked away from me, clearly not amused by my joke. He didn't look at me again until we reached the town. There weren't many trees. Everything was just rock and dirt. There was tall, brown grass that almost looked dead and huge rocks forming into grottos and things that could have been temples years ago. He parked the car on a little side road and got out before I had the chance.

"Are you just going to leave the car here? Like this?" I asked, scouring the surroundings. No one was there.

"Yes, I am," he murmured, opening the trunk and pulling out my suitcase, and my box of paints.

"Won't it be taken away?"

"I'll just get another one if I ever need to," he said with a smile. "It's not like these monetary, mundane things are difficult for someone like me."

I also got out of the car, my heart racing faster and faster as I slowly followed him toward the white rocks that led to the blue sea. It was beautiful— another painting that I wanted to capture. As I walked, I became very aware of my sore feet. At least, they were a bit better now.

"Are we going out… into the ocean?" I asked, hesitating as he inched closer and closer to the shoreline.

Down on the other side of the hill, I could see a small lighthouse that looked deserted. I wanted to ask him if I could go explore it, anything to delay what was going to happen, but I already knew that he was in a rush. I could tell by the way he was walking so fast, or it could have been that he didn't want to be seen by anyone.

"Can you keep up?" He called back over his shoulder, stopping for a moment to see how far behind I was. I saw his eyes on my feet, and I knew that he was concerned, yet stressed. His facial expression spoke volumes; he wanted me to move faster, and yet it was as if he felt bad for me. It had been my entire fault. I dashed to close the distance between us, despite the sharp pain that shot up my legs.

"How much farther do we have to go?" I asked, lifting my hand to block the sun out of my face.

"Just a few more feet down the hill, not much farther," he said, pointing toward a flat part of the hill. I could see there was a slab of concrete with an ancient Greek design on it. He walked to the giant slab in only a few steps. Every step that his long legs took, I was taking two.

"This is it?" I asked, glancing at the white, stony beach and the crystal blue water.

"The gates are underneath this," he said, putting my suitcase and my box down onto the white stones.

"Then, how are we going to get in there?" I asked.

I watched as he lifted his hands over the concrete and slowly began to spread his arms apart. As he did, the ground began to quiver, and the concrete slab began to pulse and slowly move apart. I tried to dig my heels into the stones, but I kept stumbling as the little parts of the rocks began to stumble near my feet. He stopped his arms just as there was a big enough hole for the both of us to jump down through. I had expected a sort of staircase to await us, but there was nothing but a big vast of nothing below, and the faint sound of water.

"Ladies first," he motioned toward the hole. I froze, staring at him. My heart was beating, and I glanced around the beach, taking in the sunshine one last time.

"Age before beauty," I shot back at him. Humor. Humor was always good.

"Summer," he warned, his face tensing.

"I really don't want to go down there," I whispered, trying to keep the fear out of my voice.

"It's the only way," he said with a grin, motioning toward the hole again. "The only way into the Underworld is through caves. This is the only one that isn't around crowded civilization. So, please, be brave and jump."

I knew this was it. I had no choice. If I ran away again, he'd catch me, or someone would catch me and bring me back to him. "I-I can't," I stuttered, shaking my head, backing away from the hole slowly. I watched as he walked toward me, and grabbed my wrist gently to drag me toward the black hole.

"Summer, when are you going to learn to just trust me?"

He walked me closer to the hole until I was practically looking down it. I could see the blue ocean water flowing in and out of the cavern below. I felt better knowing that it wasn't a bottomless hole, but it didn't help any that I still had to jump.

"All you have to do is jump into the water. I promise it won't hurt, and you'll be able to stand up. That's why I told you to dress for climbing." He was right. That morning, he tossed me one of my old shirts that I loved and told me to keep my paint-smudged shorts on. "We'll be climbing today," he told me. But I hadn't imagined this. "So on the count of three, you're going to jump. And then I'll toss down your stuff, and then I'll be joining you."

"You promise you'll be right behind me? That nothing horrible will happen to me when I jump?" I asked as I looked at him concerned. I was so scared, so nervous that I didn't know what to think. He smiled and shook his head.

"That would be rather pointless for me not to follow, now wouldn't it?" he said with a laugh. I gulped; hoping that counting to five would, at least, calm my nerves. It didn't.

"How far down is it?" I stammered, trying to delay.

"About fifteen feet. If you're worried about breaking your legs, you won't. Where you're jumping in, the water is about six feet. If you swim a little to your right after that, you'll be in waist deep water in minutes."

I wasn't sure if I should nod or shake my head profusely and tell him that there was no way in hell I was going down there by myself.

"One…" he began, squeezing my hand for a moment and then letting my hand drop.

"Two…" I whispered, trying to gather the last of my strength and courage.

"Three."

I didn't move. Nothing happened. He stared at me and sighed.

"Really? You were supposed to jump."

"I'm not crazy. I'm not jumping."

"Persephone didn't jump either," he mumbled, and I glared at him.

"Well, good thing I'm not Persephone," I snapped, bracing myself, and jumped. My scream the whole way down was the only thing that reminded me that I was still alive. As I crashed into the cold sea water, I could still hear the echo of my scream throughout the caverns.

"I'm sure the whole Underworld heard that scream," he laughed. His voice bounced against the walls of the cave. I swam to the right, just as he said, and felt for the bottom. It only took moments before I was standing up, hating the wet clinginess of my clothes. I pushed back my tangled hair and glanced up at the last glimmer of daylight.

"Be careful of your suitcase," he called, tossing it down into the water. I grabbed the handle and tugged it toward me. My feet were cold, and the rocks under me were slippery. I couldn't see anything. Everything around me was dark and night and cold.

"Are you coming?" I shouted, hearing my voice bounce all around me, over and over again.

"Hasty are we?" he laughed down at me. I shivered, gazing all around me again, hearing only the echoes of our voices and the slight roar of the waves. I heard him grunt a little and then there was a splash next to me, spraying more sea water into my eyes. It burned like hell.

"Are you okay?" he asked me, dashing to my side as I wiped the water away as best as I could.

"You should aim your landings a little bit better. You're a God, it should be perfect," I mumbled as I tried to open my eyes to glare at him. "Do you have my box?"

"Yes, I have it. I didn't forget," he murmured softly, touching my back with his fingers. "Can you hold onto it as I close the hole up?"

"Do you have to do that? It's going to get dark in here," I said, scouring the dark caves again, even though my eyes were burning.

"I can't let others in here. That wouldn't be safe." He handed me my box of paints and brushes, and I watched as he extended his arms out again and slowly began to move them together. The walls of the cave shook, and I thought I was going to die. I was going to be stabbed in the heart by one of the stalactites. I watched as the hole became smaller and smaller until there wasn't a ray of light left.

"Where are you?" I gasped as the dark consumed me. I couldn't even see my hand in front of me.

"It's alright; I'm right here," he whispered, grabbing my elbow. I felt him take the box out of my hand, pulling me to his side. Out of the corner of the dark cavern, I saw a small dim light coming toward us.

"What is that?" I panicked. I could hear my feet splattering in the water. I was scared.

"Calm down, everything is going to be alright," he whispered into my ear. I felt his arm wrap around my waist, and I was by his side. The air was getting thicker and moist and didn't smell as sweet as the summer air above did. It smelled of death.

"What is that light?" I whispered again, watching it slowly become bigger and brighter.

"That is Charon," he murmured. "Do you know who Charon is?"

I watched as the eerie black boat came closer. I could even hear the swishing of the water that Charon was making with his oar.

"Yes," I whispered. "I know who Charon is."

"Good, then. I don't have to make an introduction," he said with a smirk. The boat stopped in front of us, and I took in how empty and large it was. The oars on the side stood straight up in the air, and I couldn't help but look around the cavern. Where had he gone?

"Greetings, my lord," a faint deep voice echoed throughout the cave. Hades smiled and lifted himself into the vessel.

"Hello, Charon."

"You found the girl," the voice was like a gruff whisper heard in horror films and the hair on my arms stood up in reaction.

"Yes. This is Summer." Hades gazed at me and lifted his hand out toward me. I handed him my box of paints and lifted myself into the black boat. It felt slimy, like wet rocks at the bottom of a lake. I wanted to wipe my hands on my jeans, but I knew that it wouldn't help any. I wrapped my arms around myself and tried to warm my body. The cavern was cold, and my wet jeans weren't helping the situation of trying to stay warm.

"Home, Charon. Please." I felt the boat shift, and slowly turn in the narrow canal, and the oar that stood straight up began to move on its own.

"Where is he?" I whispered, leaning into Hades' warmth. He turned and smiled.

"You can't see him?"

I shook my head, staring at the oar as it began to lift and move the boat forward a bit faster through the tunnel of darkness. I slipped my hand around his arm, and I pulled myself closer to him. The caves got darker, and I knew I was getting farther and farther away from the normal world. His arm wrapped around my waist, and I felt safe—secure, even though I didn't want to be that close to him.

Everything was dark and unfamiliar. His arm squeezed me a little tighter as we descended farther and farther into the caves. I wondered where we were in relation to the world above us. I couldn't see where he was taking me, but in my heart I already knew. I knew what was coming. I had imagined the setting of the Underworld. It would be dark, and the air wouldn't be as crisp as it was above us. There were tunnels and caves that led to other tunnels and caves, all dark, all silent, and all dead.

"Are you afraid?" he whispered, his chilling breath on my neck.

"A little." I shivered. He stopped, and I could finally see a dim light ahead of us. It was a pinkish glow, something that I had only ever seen in horror films. I should have expected things like that here. This was the palace of horrors.

"I want to warn you just ahead of us is a lair in which all the souls live. You might see things that you might find unsettling."

I nodded, wanting to close my eyes. I wished that this was just some awful haunted house ride and that I could just get off at the end of the tunnel and go back into daylight. But this ride had no good ending. This was only the beginning. My eyes began to scan the water. It was dark. Black. There was no end or beginning to the water and the rocks. The pink glow began to emanate from the water around us, and I knew what that light was from. The light of souls. The orbs began to grow in numbers until we were completely surrounded. I could hear moans and cries. I felt a throbbing in my heart. Were my parents here? Was my father now an orb in this black river? I wanted to lean down and touch one. I wanted to see what would happen. I felt myself leaning closer and closer to the slimy boat's edge.

"No!" I felt him pull me back and pulled my chin so that I looked him in the eye. "You cannot touch them. Do not disturb the souls."

"I didn't mean to…"

"Don't." He interrupted. I felt myself shiver again, and I nodded solemnly.

"Can I ask why?"

"Would you want to be disturbed?" He answered harshly. I didn't reply.

The oars changed its course, and we went toward a narrow cave. I knew what was coming next. We'd have to go by Cerberus. The watchdog that let everyone into the Underworld Kingdom, but never lets anyone out. Hades sat silently beside me, glancing around the dark ruins of his home. Was he happy to be home? I didn't know how he could prefer this to the world above. I closed my eyes, wanting to just wait until we hit dry land to see the horrors that remained, but the loud bark of his dog jolted me and forced me to look forward.

"Silence!" the deeply echoed voice of Charon shouted, and I watched as the large, black, three-headed dog stepped back, eyeing me carefully.

"Welcome to the Asphodel Meadows," he whispered. The cave became a forest of grass and flowers and trees. It almost looked like home. The light in the caverns was coming from the orbs that floated around the grassy pastures.

"It's beautiful here."

"This is where everyone goes. Not the good or the bad." I saw that the river ended, and I knew that we'd have to journey the rest of the way on foot.

"Are your feet alright?" he asked gently as the boat docked and he lifted himself and a suitcase out of the boat. I nodded and followed him quickly, wanting to escape the invisible eyes of Charon.

"Thank you, Charon. That will be all." The boat's oar rose from the water and began its journey back through the narrow cave. I could already hear Cerberus's bark echo around me.

"The palace is ahead. Follow me." I did as he told, and I kept close behind him, watching my step as I glanced around. Had Persephone been frightened, as he led her through here the first time? It all felt so familiar; the way the trees bent over the trail, the way the grass moved in the cold breeze from the water. I was Odette, following the winged, dark shadow of Rothbart, towards his grim underworld palace of death; and there was no moonlight or Prince to save me.

Chapter Fourteen

My eyes dashed over my surroundings, remembering the jump and the journey on Charon's boat, the orbs and the smell. The room was small, and it looked ancient; like something I would have found in one of my Greek Mythology books back in my room, in that place that felt so far away now. The bed was white; the sheets were white with gold embroidery around the edges. Orchids in a vase sat alone on a side table. I knew in my heart this was her room. He had put me in her room. I looked down at my clothes, hoping that there was still some normalcy to me, but even those remnants of my past life were gone. I couldn't remember how I came to be in this room. Everything was a blur in my mind. How long had I been there? A day? A couple of days? A week? I pulled the white sheets away, feeling the stickiness peel away with them. I took a peek at my feet and saw they looked almost healed. I touched a scabbed part on my heel and didn't feel any pain anymore.

I pushed myself out of bed, testing my feet and realizing that I would be all right to walk, and moved to my suitcase that sat on an old chair. I knew that I shouldn't expect to find my old clothing in there, but I hoped. I pulled open the top and found dresses that I hadn't remembered packing. They looked old fashioned and silky. Definitely not me. I glanced around the room again, feeling my breath quicken. Anger and panic filled my chest, and I couldn't breathe. I pushed myself back onto the bed and closed my eyes, counting to ten. Everything would be okay. Everything was going to be okay.

"Good morning," his voice was soft as he entered my room. I saw him enter through another doorway on the other side of the room, but I quickly darted my gaze away; I didn't want to look at him.

"Where are my clothes?" I demanded.

"Don't you like those?" I saw his shadowy form walk across the room to my suitcase, where he lifted a yellow, silky dress and brought it toward me. His hands startled me. He looked different. My eyes moved up his body. His skin was different, full of shadows and ancient design.

"Do you have tattoos?"

"They're not exactly tattoos."

"What is it then?" I asked, glancing up at his face.

"It's a sign that I'm a God. We all have these markings."

"Why didn't I see it before?" I asked, gently grazing my finger over his hardened arm. I felt his body tense, and I looked back up at him.

"I couldn't very well walk around like this and blend in with everyone, now could I?" The lines on his body were moving. They were in a never-ending battle to dominate a portion of his body. I started to notice the differences between his human form, and his God form. His hair was fuller now, less stringy. It was jet black and beautiful. His eyes had particles of black and green. He looked like a God. A true God.

"Can I have my clothes back?"

"You don't need them here," he murmured, holding out the yellow dress to me. "I had a collection of things sent to you. I wish for you to wear them."

"Not only do you want me to be the part, but dress the part now, too?"

"There is going to be a welcoming celebration for you this evening."

"I'm not going to any celebration. I don't want to celebrate. I have nothing to celebrate," I snapped, pushing the dress into his chest. "You can wear the dresses yourself," I finished, pushing myself farther into the bed and pulling the covers over my head. "I don't want to play dress up with you." I felt a shift in the bed, and suddenly the blankets were off of me.

"No. You will do as I ask."

"You have no authority over me."

"I have all authority over you. You are in my domain now. I have said in everything," he snapped as he pulled me out of the bed and toward the suitcase.

"You *will* wear this, Summer. You will. You will do what I ask."

"Why? Why should I? You take me away from everything that I know. Everything that I love, and then expect me to be your doll. I'm not your plaything, and I am not Persephone anymore. She's gone."

"No. I refuse to accept that." He tossed the dress into my arms and began walking toward the door that he came through.

"You will dress in that, and you will come to the celebration tonight. I'll drag you by the hair if I have to," he thundered, and I felt the pang of fear shiver down my spine.

His anger echoed through the designs on his skin, and with a roar of rage, he slammed the door. I felt so desperate. I needed air. I felt like I couldn't catch my breath. I let the dress fall from my arms and I sunk to the floor. I glanced at the arm where he grabbed me and noticed the dark marks that traced along my skin.

"The dark marks mean you are mine." The voice echoed in my thoughts over and over again until I couldn't think anymore. I felt the urge to cry, but no tears came. I had cried so much within the last few days that my body couldn't produce any more tears; nor did he deserve them.

I glanced at the dress and knew what I had to do. I pulled it closer to me, tracing the silk with my fingertips, and slowly undressed my old form, into his false queen.

* * * *

The only light around the palace came from the tall candle sconces on the walls. He was far from any modern-day living. No wonder he liked the expensive hotels, with all the finery inside. I pulled myself along the edges of the corridors, afraid that I'd find some creature lurking just on the other side. The only thing I should have been afraid of was him. I pushed the image of him out of my mind, knowing that I would only cause myself to get more upset. I knew after this celebration; I'd search my room for my paints and take my anger out on my brushes. The palace was black. Everything was black. I stuck out like a sore thumb— the beautiful maiden in yellow, lurking about a dark castle, trying to avoid the dark king.

"I've been waiting for you," his voice startled me, and I jumped away from the wall. His black form emerged from the wall behind me, and there was a gentle smirk on his face.

"How long have you been there, watching me?"

He shrugged. "Long enough to be amused."

I didn't return his smile. Nothing could make me smile. There was a small moment of silence as he grabbed my hand and lifted it to his arm.

"Would you like to know who has come to see you?"

"Not really," I murmured. He gave me a dark look and then continued on.

"My dearest friend, Hermes has come to see you." Hermes. He was the messenger of the Gods— one of the Gods that my father liked. The thought of my father made me smile. That time felt so far away, out of my hands completely.

"And Hecate," he whispered. "You know her, correct?" Hecate. She was the Goddess of Magic and Crossroads. She existed between reality and dreams, and it was believed that she helped Persephone accept and escape the Underworld.

"I've heard of her," I whispered.

"Well, you will know her, again," he murmured. "I'm sure she's the most excited to see you."

I couldn't feel anything. My body was numb. What happened to me? To us? I glanced at Hades and felt my chest twist in fear. He was different. He wasn't the same man as he had been above. He was colder and harder. What happened to the man that was gentle? The man that was kind? I looked at his lips, wanting to feel them again. Would he be the same as he had been before? Would he be forceful?

"You're quiet," he whispered.

"Good of you to notice," I retorted. He stopped and pulled my hand gently to stop me from walking away.

"This is all for you," he replied curtly.

"Who are you talking to? For me? For Summer?" I felt the anger rush through me like a wind. I wanted to hold my breath and calm myself, but I couldn't. "Look at me," I snapped. "I'm not her. You can dress me up all you want. You can call me all kinds of sweet names or what have you, but it doesn't change anything. I'm still Summer. I'm still me. Nothing you say can change that." He stared at me for a moment and glanced down at my hand in his.

"I don't want to change anything about you," he whispered. I saw a glimpse of the old him— the old him that I stayed in the hotel rooms with for days. I brought myself closer to him. His skin almost welcomed my touch, danced around my fingertips.

"Please don't push me away," I whispered, feeling the brink of tears nearing me again. "I just can't bear to be in this place, alone. You took away the only things I had left of my life," I felt him shift, and he shook his head.

"I put them away. Just for now. They're in your room."

"And my other belongings?"

"They're under your bed. I wouldn't dare take away your paints, Summer." He stopped and lifted his eyes toward mine. "I want to make you happy. I want this place to be your new home."

My anger from earlier seemed to wash away without a trace. His eyes, his lips, his smile were all consuming, and I felt his hands pull me closer.

"I'm sorry," he murmured. "And I don't say that often."

I smiled, tucking a strand of my hair behind my ear. "I'll try my best," I whispered. He nodded, lifting his hand to my chin and gently grazed his lips on mine.

"I know who you are, Summer, but I also trust that you'll embrace who you're meant to be." With that, he gently tucked my hand onto his arm and guided me toward the main hall, where everyone was waiting to meet Persephone.

The room was large and was lit by even larger candles, all of them black. I was almost sure that the orbs that I had seen in the water were also helping to light up the room. There were three men standing off to one side of a large black chair that I already knew was his throne. There was a golden chair beside his, decorated with gold vines and flowers. I knew that had to be hers.

"Those men there," he said, lifting his hand in their direction, "are the judges." I had a vague idea of how everything happened here. The stories of the Underworld never had anything to do with anyone other than Hades for me.

"Aeacus, Minos and Rhadamanthus." Their names matched their looks. Neither of them looked normal in the least. They looked ancient with the way they composed themselves. They held the years of their life on their shoulders. Their eyes held wisdom that couldn't be spoken of; lifetimes were written in the creases on their skin. Dead - they appeared to belong to the underworld. Hades guided me toward the golden chair beside his. Her seat; his Queen.

"Please sit and endure this," he commanded softly. I watched as he stood away from me and lifted his hands toward the group of people on the dance floor in front of us. He looked like a King. His smile and posture even spoke royalty. I had never noticed until now.

"Thank you for coming to the celebration," he began. The gray figures stood and watched like ghosts. I wondered if they were ghosts. I tried to make out face features, clothes, shoes, but it was all a blur. There was one face that stood out to me the most. Whoever the man was, he looked cruel. His snarl on his mouth spoke evil. His eyes were like daggers as he gazed at me. I couldn't even focus on what Hades was saying until he said, "Please greet your Queen, for she has journeyed far to be with you," I glanced at him and knew at that moment that I couldn't pretend. I would lose at this game. If I remembered everything, I'd lose him forever. She'd win. She'd take over my body, and he'd be happy again. He'd have his real Queen. Music began to play, and the gray figures began to twirl around each other; palm to palm.

"You should join them," he murmured.

"Will you join too?" I whispered, trying to hide the fear in my voice. He smiled and motioned for me to move toward the crowd. I stood up, watching as a few of the gray figures stopped to stare as I descended toward them. A gap opened in the crowd and I saw a gray figure come toward me. I glanced at Hades as he sat on his dark throne, watching me among his dead citizens. I glimpsed back at the gray figure and saw their blood red eyes meet mine. I jumped back for a moment but felt their grip on my hand tug me into the dance.

The faces that flooded the room were grotesque, dead, and seemed to have come right out of my dream. Their red eyes sent a shrill of fear down my spine. The pace of the music around the room kept the movement as lively as it could have been. It sounded like music that I would have heard in a Jane Austen movie. Each palm rose up to meet mine as they twirled me in circles. I could hear her name on their lips, and it angered me. I wanted to correct them. I wasn't Persephone.

"You look so happy to be back, my lady," a man whispered as his palm touched mine. I could taste the sarcasm in his voice. I felt his cold hand touch the base of my back and pulled me away from the large crowd of dancers. I felt dizzy and relieved at once to be rescued from all the spinning and the red eyes.

"I'm Thanatos." The man's smile was evil. It sent a chill right through my skin. His dirty brown hair fell over the left side of his face, and down his shoulders. He was dressed just like everyone else; all in black. Thanatos. Demon of Death. He was death personified. I felt his fingers touch mine for a brief moment, and he smiled.

"Let's be honest, my lady, shall we? We both know that you're not who my lord says you are."

"I've never denied that," I whispered.

"So you admit that you're not really Persephone?" His smile widened, and I felt a chill run down my body. He began to circle me, the same way I had imagined sharks circled their prey. I closed my eyes, wanting nothing more than to run to the white room with silk sheets. It might not have been home, but it was safety. I couldn't trust anyone here. I was reminded of how alone I was. "You're human," he whispered into my ear, and I felt the hairs on my neck stand. "You'll never escape this place, Summer. You'll die here. You're human. You're a meal to us. We'll suck your soul right out of you," he sneered.

"I have the protection of Hades," I tried, glancing at him as he sat on his throne. He was busy talking to one of the old judges. I wished for a moment he would look my way.

"Only for so long, my sweet. Once he realizes who you'll never be, he'll let the Underworld eat you up. It won't be long until the Fates come and cut your line."

I knew there was promise in his voice, and he was right. I remembered who he was from the stories that my father told me. Thanatos used to make the decision of who would die until Hades tricked him and brought him here. He was a victim, just like me.

"So, you can either give up the act now," he began, "Or you..."

"I'm not acting. If you think, I want to be here…" I tried to interject, but he lifted a cold finger to my lips, shaking his head.

"Why don't you just leave then?" he asked softly, glancing around. "No one is watching."

"I can't. No one can leave this place."

His eyebrow rose as he gave me another cruel smile. "I might be able to arrange something for you," he said, twirling the ends of his hair between his fingers.

I knew there had to be a catch. He seemed like the kind of person that didn't just give things away for free, especially freedom.

"There is a woman, who might be able to help you, Summer. Have you heard of the maiden's mother?"

"Are you talking about Demeter?" I asked my eyes wide.

"How silly of me, of course you know who she is," he said with a controlled laugh. He began to circle around me again. The shark after his prey. "You know her better than you probably know." I didn't understand what he meant, but I didn't want to ask. For once, I was going to hold my tongue and keep myself out of more trouble.

"Do you know how Persephone got away from my lord?" He asked an amused look on his face as he watched me.

"She was stolen away by Zeus, and her mother," I replied, shrugging slightly.

"Yes, she was stolen away, sort of. But she ate a few tiny seeds. She promised a few months out of her life every year to come back and be with him, but for the rest of the remaining time, she was free."

"I'm not Persephone, and that's not going to happen to me." I snapped, shaking my head. I tried to escape his circling form, but he grabbed my arm and glanced down at my wrist.

"How do you know it hasn't already?" He sneered, keeping his gaze latched to mine. "The seeds that you ate at home?" He questioned, nodding as the distant images crossed my memory. The pomegranate in the fridge at home. Was that him? Had he already tricked me into this repeat of history? How did Thanatos know this?

"See this?" he tapped the bruise that was taking shape on my arm. "He's already made his mark on you."

"It's a bruise," I retorted, pulling my arm away from him. "You wouldn't know anything about those since you're not human."

"He won't stop there, my sweet. He's had you from day one when he discovered your paintings. The moment he knew that you dreamt of him, he had this foolish idea that Persephone still existed in your mind. I think it's impossible."

"It's not impossible," I whispered. "She's very much alive in me."

"Then why not give the master what he wants?" He sneered. "You'd be doing yourself a great favor."

I was speechless. Should I tell him the truth? Should I tell him about my feelings? The look that he gave me told me that he already knew.

"You love him, don't you?" He laughed. He glanced at Hades and then back at me. "Oh, what a fool you are, Summer."

"What does it matter?" I snapped, wanting to escape. I tried to glance around the room, but he pulled me in front of him. His eyes were hard and serious.

"He will never love you, Summer. He will only ever love the woman within you."

"I refuse to accept that," I snarled. "There has to be something about me, just me that he loves."

"I hate to disappoint you, my sweet, but it's very much true. Hades cannot love. Not anymore."

I pushed his hands off of my arms and managed to take a few steps back. Thanatos laughed, and grabbed my hand, lifting it up to his lips.

"Good evening, my lady." He pushed himself through the haze of gray figures and left me to stand, surrounded by their glowing, red eyes. I was living my nightmare. I closed my eyes, trying to bring reality back. This had to be a dream. I was probably still sleeping in my bed at home, in Point Judith, or even in one of the hotels in Greece. Anyplace, but here.

I felt a hand touch my elbow, and I jolted back. My eyes widened as a kind face greeted mine. It was far from what I expected. The kind face belonged to a woman, who had long, dark brown hair. It was curly and wild. Her eyes were deep and silver, almost like moons. I felt as if I had known her from somewhere, but the memory was too far away. Her eyes were soft as she smiled at me and took my hand, tracing her fingertips over my bruise. I watched as it began to blend into my skin until it was completely gone. I noticed a gold band around her head that probably symbolized some sort of power or rank. I tried to go through lists of names of Goddesses that my mother had taught me, but I knew most of them couldn't ever come to the Underworld. They'd never be able to leave this place.

"I'm Hecate," she whispered with a smile. She must have read the confusion in my eyes. I gave her a small smile, wanting to pull my arm out of her grasp. I wanted to just go back to my room. *I'm not here to harm you*; she said the words in my mind. My eyes widened as I watched her lips stay firm and unmoving. *I'm here to protect you, Summer. I knew your mother*. The voice seemed to echo through my head, over and over again.

My mother? Did she really mean *my* mother? "My mother?" I asked aloud, shocked. My mother knew Hecate?

How could that even be possible? Hecate's eyes dashed toward Hades and then back at me.

"We cannot speak here like this," she whispered in reply, shaking her head. "There is much that you don't know. Everything will begin to reveal itself soon." She gently let go of my arm and touched my cheek for a moment. *You are safe here*. The echo in my mind made my body relax for a moment.

I gave her a small smile and nodded. I lowered my eyes to my arm, noticing the hint of glow coming from the area of the bruise. It was unusually bright.

"What are you doing over here alone?" I glanced up at the sound of his voice and pushed my arm behind my back. The woman was gone, and the gray figures around me were behind Hades. His eyes were hard again, a fire raging inside. I wanted to touch him and soften it. I knew I had to say the right thing.

"Just waiting for you to join me," I murmured.

His hand tucked a strand of my hair behind my ear and brushed against my cheek. "Are you ready to go to bed?"

"Can I talk to you alone?" I managed, glancing up at him. He nodded, giving me a curt smile. I followed him through the crowd of gray figures, keeping my eyes downcast so I wouldn't have to see their glowing eyes. They were the soul eaters. I knew it. I wanted to close myself off completely and keep everything intact, even if death was lurking just around the corner.

* * * *

"She knew my mother," I whispered into his shoulder. Hades was lying beside me in the large, white bed. I felt the need to be held, even if it was by him. I had no one else to love me. Everything that I knew was gone. Everything that I loved was gone, except him. I was curled into his side, wishing that we were still in my world. I missed the sounds of cars and airplanes, the assurance of a light switch or the dim red lights of an alarm clock. There was nothing but blackness here.

"Who?" he whispered. He turned his head to look at me.

"Hecate." There was a thick silence between us for a moment. It could have been that I imagined it, but I could almost picture his pursing lips.

"I didn't see you talking to her," he stated flatly.

"Did she know my mother?" I asked as I lifted my head onto my hand, digging my elbow into the sheets. He turned his body toward me, mimicking my movements.

"It doesn't matter, does it?"

"If she knew my mother, who else did?" I exclaimed, shoving a hand into his chest.

His chest was hard and warm. I remembered the first time I had felt his chest. My room was a place that didn't even exist anymore, and I knew it was useless to think about. All that mattered was my survival here, in the Underworld. I had my first real enemy, and it was Death. What a great way of starting out in a new place.

"Are you sure she wasn't talking about Demeter? To the crowd, you were Persephone."

I closed my eyes and tried to remember her words. I knew she had spoken my name. She had addressed me as Summer, which only could mean she knew *my* mother.

I'm here to protect you, Summer. I knew your mother. What did it all mean?

"She called me Summer," I whispered. "She meant my mother." I felt Hades tense and pull away from me. I didn't watch him sit up and move toward the door that he came in from. I knew he was hiding something, and I knew he wouldn't tell me. It would be the same old answers. I had to find everything out for myself, and I was determined.

Chapter Fifteen

The kitchen looked the same way I left it. My painting was still hanging on the wall. The pale yellow wallpaper was starting to peel, though. The kitchen table was dusty, and my fingertips gathered the gray substance as they skimmed over the wood. I knew that if we were still living here, the kitchen wouldn't look this way. I felt my stomach growl, and I wondered if I'd find moldy food in the fridge. My footsteps felt heavy with every step that I took. It felt like I was walking through deep water.

I opened the door and felt the cold air graze over my face. It felt different— almost like a familiar breath on my neck. There was a hunk of cheese sitting on the top shelf with fragments of stick butter. Why hadn't my mother thrown these out? I pushed aside a few jars of unopened pickles and olives until I found a red fruit that caught my eye. I knew this fruit. My mouth watered as I pulled it out of the fridge. I watched my hands break it apart, the red juice staining my skin as it dripped onto the floor. I pushed two fingers into the broken skin and brought a seed out, lifting it to my lips. I stared at the seed in between my fingers. I could accept my fate and eat the seed, or fight.

Be free, the seed whispered to me. It taunted me. *Be happy. Be with him. Let Persephone come home to him. Be free.* I glanced around the kitchen, wanting an escape, but the doors were gone. The room was getting smaller and smaller, the air tighter and humid. The painting on the wall was different. The garden was gone. The mother was gone. Hades stood proudly, extending a pomegranate in his hand, toward the girl. The girl who looked more like me, then the blonde goddess that I had painted.

"Choose me," he whispered. The crunch of the seed in my mouth jolted me awake.

I sat up, pushing the sticky blankets off of me, and pulled my hands through my damp hair. I wanted to be free of the dreams. I wanted to find the meanings behind them and then let them all go. I searched my room for a distraction in the darkness, but nothing seemed to stand out. I pushed myself off of my bed and pulled one of the flowing dresses out of the suitcase that was still sitting against a wall. It glided over my skin. Silk.

I didn't want to see my reflection, too afraid of what I would find reflected back. Would I see her smiling face looking back at mine? I moved toward the door as fast as I could. I wanted relief, air, an escape, anything. I pushed myself down the dark hallway as quietly as I could. The candles on the wall flickered as I moved past them. I imagined a haunted house with paintings littering the walls, and as the unsuspecting visitor moved by them, the eyes of the painting would follow them. I glanced behind me, making sure that no one was following me. I wanted alone time; the time that I hadn't had ever since the accident. The corridor led to the grand hall we danced in the night before. At the far end, there were two large doors. I raced across the dance floor, pushing aside the images of all that happened there; the ghosts, the eyes, and Thanatos. I had hesitated before I pulled on one of the large door handles. It took all my strength to crack it open to peek beyond the thick wood.

"What are you doing over there?" I heard the sickeningly familiar snicker, and I turned around to see Thanatos smiling at me. He slowly emerged out of the shadows of the hall like a snake with a large smile on his face. "Exploring are we?"

"It is my new home. I have every right," I snapped.

"Curiosity killed the cat. I would know," he said with a laugh and started to walk toward me, filling in the space between us. "I think perhaps, we got off on the wrong foot," He said, lifting his fingers to his lips. I began to back up against the door. I didn't want to feel his cold touch on my skin, and I knew he would try.

"I don't think so," I whispered.

"You dislike me," he sighed. "Though, it shouldn't surprise me. Most don't like me." He stopped until he was right in front of me. I could almost feel his breath on my face. I could see the glimmer of pleasure in his eye at my discomfort. "Do you want to know what lies behind this door?" He motioned toward the door. I didn't want to admit how curious I was.

"The River Lethe begins here," he whispered as he placed a hand near my shoulder, grabbing the door handle.

I slipped away before he could get any closer to me. I watched as he slowly opened the door without any effort. "You do know about the Lethe, right?"

"It's the river of forgetfulness," I whispered.

"Yes, that's right," He said with a smile. He motioned for me to go through the doorway. "Most spirits use this river to forget their past lives before they are reincarnated. Some others use it to forget so that their time here in the Underworld isn't torturous." The dark cave smelled of sulfur and there seemed to be a faint, sanitized scent of chlorine. It made my head hurt. I felt his cold, clammy hand grab mine and he pulled me into the cave until it opened to a large, gray sky. "If you look just ahead, you'll see the spirits bathing here."

I didn't want to watch, but my mouth couldn't open. My voice wasn't working. The stench seemed to paralyze me. I could see gray forms in the distance splashing the black water around them.

"There's a rumor floating around the Gods that Demeter poisoned her daughter with Lethe waters. It seems that if it is true, Persephone had some stronger powers than most thought. You remember things, don't you Summer? You just can't piece it together yet."

"There's nothing to piece together," I managed between a gasp of breath.

"Are you still going on like that? The Lord won't be happy to hear you speak like this."

"The 'Lord' won't care. I can guarantee you that." My lungs hurt as I breathed my words. My head was spinning, and my ears were ringing. This place was deadly for me. I felt his fingers grab my arms, and his fingernails dig into my skin.

"Oh, he will care, my dear. More so than you can imagine."

"He doesn't tell me anything!" I shouted. My words echoed around me, rung in my ears. I knew the gray forms heard me. I could feel it, and they were crawling to us. They wanted relief like I did.

"If he finds you useless, he'll let death find you."

"It seems that death has already found me. It's standing right in front of me," I retorted. My lungs were on fire. I was holding back the pain.

"If you do not remember and accept who you are, you will die here. You will be here forever."

"I don't care," I whispered. I wanted to die. I wanted to be free.

"You're already dying if you didn't already know that. Not even Hades can save you. You can never return home. You'll die here, and then you'll be just like them," he replied with a smile. "You could always take a sip of the water, and you could forget who you are. Maybe Persephone could truly come alive then. My Lord could have what he wishes, and you wouldn't suffer."

He turned toward the black water and knelt down beside it. His fingers grazed the top of the surface. I could see the gray forms coming closer to him. I backed away from him, pushing myself toward the door. He watched me and lifted his hand, motioning for me to come to him. I heard the door behind me close. I knew that I couldn't open that door by myself.

"Where do you think you're going?"

"I'm not going to drink anything," I murmured, pushing myself against the wooden door behind me.

"Oh, yes you are," he said amused. "It'll be the solution to all of your problems, my dear."

"No," I shook my head. "No, it won't."

I watched him dip his hand into the black water and make a cup. He slowly stood up, bringing it toward me. I had nowhere else to go.

"You want freedom, and here it is," He whispered with a smile.

"That's not freedom. Not real freedom."

"A form of freedom, my love," he smiled. I grabbed his wrist, pushing it toward his chest. I didn't want it. I didn't want to know the taste of death. I wanted to find Hades. I wished he'd barge in and find Thanatos and make him drink it.

"It's not good enough."

"I'm afraid that you'll never find anything to your liking here. Not until you finally let everything from your old life go." His hand drifted up toward my lips, my hand weakening.

"That's never going to happen," I whispered.

"And so, you'll never be happy. Do you really want to spend the rest of your life so unhappy here? Drinking this would solve everything. He would be happy; you would be happy…"

"Or so you like to think." I retorted, shoving his hand back. The water droplets plummeted from his hand, and he hissed.

"There isn't enough room for you here," he sneered.

I felt a chill in the air that almost crawled up my skin. I could tell by Thanatos's face that whoever had caused the chill in the air, they scared him. I slowly began to turn around, hoping to see his face. I wanted nothing more than to catch his familiar eyes. I wondered what I'd find there if I'd find anything at all. Instead, I saw her standing behind me. Her wild hair was whipping in the cool air, and her eyes were ice. I could almost imagine winter in those silver eyes. The tall pine trees, covered with icicles dripping off of them like tear drops.

"What are you doing here, Thanatos?" Her voice reflected the same image. I could imagine the snow falling around us. It felt safe; nothing that I needed to be afraid of.

"Lethe is more powerful than you give it credit for, my dear," he whispered. "It could be the answer to everything if you would only let it."

"And what do you think he'd say if he found out what you would have done?"

"He'd be proud." His chin almost rose with the answer. The arrogance seeped out of him like a pool of green ooze. I felt the desire to shove him backward into that deathly river.

"If you took her memories, there would be nothing left of her."

"You miss nothing, do you?" His lips rose in a small smile.

"You have no right to be here, Thanatos. You anger the spirits as much as you do me. This is a sacred place. These waters are only meant for the spirits. Not for your cruelty," Hecate roared.

"What you are doing to her now is just as cruel," he whispered as he began to walk towards her and me. My breath hitched. "She'll never be what he wants. *She* is gone. Dead. Like the rest of everything here. And she will die too. Everything is pointless."

I lowered my head, keeping my eyes on my feet. I couldn't bear the thought of death, let alone my own, and he talked about it so effortlessly. Death meant nothing to him.

"The only meaningless thing is you," she whispered. I watched him grimace, and he slowly began to walk away.

"We're not through, my pet," he whispered to me as he brushed by me. I could feel the lurch of tears, but I tried to hold them back. I tried to think of anything that wasn't dark or didn't belong to this place, but my mind was filled with the cobwebs of the Underworld. I was becoming a part of this place.

Hecate turned and extended her hand to me. "He has no power here, and he has no right to harm you. You are under Hades' protection," she murmured as she began to slowly turn away, and go back the way she came.

"Wait," I whispered, lifting my hand to stop her as if I held some magic in my fingertips. Hecate turned for a moment, looking into my eyes, giving me a silent answer. I was safe. That was all I needed to know. Everything else would fall into place. My questions were meant to be answered another time.

My feet began to move before my mind allowed them. I was running through the door, away from the black souls, their red eyes, and their sticky hands. I ran away into the palace, like the locked princess I knew I was becoming, and hid away in my room. I laid on the white bed and watched the shadows of the day pass along my walls. I wasn't sure if they were real shadows or souls, watching me, waiting to see if I would try to escape. Even if there was a way out, I didn't know how to get to it. I knew that no one here was on my side. I was on my own.

Chapter Sixteen

"You weren't at dinner." I heard his voice before I saw his disgruntled face. The lack of my presence must have annoyed him or worried him. I turned my sleep-filled body toward his voice and found his face leaning over the bed sheets.

"I fell asleep," I murmured, brushing my brown hair out of my face and met his gaze. It was dark and unfamiliar. I felt a twisting pain in my heart at the sight. I wanted the man that had come for me. Was that strange to say? The man in front of me was a stranger. He was crueler than before, distant. I wanted to ask him where he had been all day. But I didn't want to hear about souls and death.

"What did you do today?" I watched his face change once he noticed my steady gaze. His dark hair brushed over his eyes as he sat closer to me. I wasn't sure if I should tell him about Thanatos and his intentions toward me. I felt like I should have been able to handle it better, but everything was going wrong here. This place was not the way I had imagined it to be.

"I took a little walk," I whispered, bringing myself back to the conversation. I felt his fingers touch mine, and I glanced down at his pale hands. I had so many questions to ask him since the occurrence at the river, but I didn't know how to ask them. I didn't want to hear the truth of Thanatos' words. Would he really let death take me? Was I really dying?

"Did you enjoy yourself?" His voice was calm. He couldn't have known what happened.

"I suppose," I said, keeping the truth inside of me. I could feel it crawl in my stomach. I wanted to tell him about what I saw. The river, the spirits and how Hecate had saved me. The truth was brimming into my mouth, and I knew that if I opened my lips, it would spill out.

"Would you like me to have dinner brought to you?" he murmured, glancing around the white room. I waited until the silence brought his gaze back to me, and I slowly shook my head. "Are you alright?" His voice was full of concern, and I could see it on the curve of his eyebrow. He wanted the truth. He could tell I was lying. For a moment, it was the same way that it had been before. His concern was familiar, the tone of his voice like a whisper in my ear. I could see him sitting in the chair in the corner of the dark hotel room while I lay in bed.

"What would you do with me, if I couldn't remember?" The question spilled out, but I closed my lips before any more could fill the room.

He was silent for a moment, and then slowly turned toward me. "What does it matter? You will remember. You already are."

"Would you kill me?" I pressed on. I had to know.

I watched his lips curve into a slight smile. "I wouldn't let anything hurt you, Summer. Nothing. Not even me."

"Would you let me go?" I knew that I had nothing to go back to. Home was nowhere. There was nothing left for me if he ever did decide to return me to the world above. Everything that I loved was gone. I watched him slowly nod and then glance at me.

"I suppose I could. Do you not like your home here?"

"I miss my home. My world."

He slowly nodded and sighed. "That isn't the first time I've heard that. Sometimes I wonder if I did the right thing," he whispered, keeping his eyes on the white sheets. I felt the boundaries between us slowly disappearing again like they had in the hotel rooms above. I didn't want him to close me off anymore. I wanted to slip under his skin and belong. I wanted to know what he was thinking and feeling every day, every minute. As much as I wanted to be free, and home, I knew that I would always want to return, to be right here with him. I wondered what he saw when he looked at me now. Did he still see Persephone?

"What do you mean?"

"Taking you away from everything. Bringing you here. I brought you here for what? To tell me what happened to a woman that disappeared thousands of years ago. I was never meant for something as real as her."

I sucked in a deep breath, shocked by his sudden candidness. Since when did he express any deep feelings toward me? I slowly began to move my body toward the edge of the bed, closer and closer to him. I wanted to reach my hand out to him and have him look at me the same way he did in the hotel room days ago. I wanted his lips on mine. I wanted him. I wanted to be someone that was real as Persephone had been to him. It didn't even matter anymore that I was from another time, another place. I was the same heart that she was. I was the one with the mind and the body to love him now. It was my turn.

"Could you," I began. "Could you ever think to love me? Just as me?" I didn't know why my lips had to open, revealing my inner war. Maybe his sudden honesty reminded me to do the same. I felt like I had just spilled a gallon of red paint all over a white canvas. There was no way I could ever get the white to be as pure as it had been moments ago.

He turned slowly to gaze at me with eyes that were empty. Hollow. His black hair fell into his face, and his jaw was clenched. There was something distant that I couldn't reach. I touched his cheek as he came closer to me. My touch almost seemed to unlock something that was still alive in him. There weren't words for what his eyes suddenly exposed for a moment. There was regret and sadness and yearning. He yearned for something that I could give him— that I wanted to give him.

His hands found mine, and his body was on me. His lips crushed onto mine as if I were his air. I was giving him life, and he wanted to take it all. I was lost in a sea of black and night and his body. I wondered for a moment how this would look with paints. Would I ever be able to take a brush and paint what I imagined now? His lips splashed colors behind my eyelids, almost as if he heard my thoughts, and wanted to help to create a painting I'd never forget. His hands moved up my shoulders and my neck, touching my lips, my fingers, and my stomach. I could only feel the colors come out of his fingertips as he traced them over me entirely. I felt as if I was his canvas and he was telling a story.

Once there was a girl, who loved a man who wasn't real. Then he came to her, took her away and wanted to love her. Wanted to love someone that was inside of her. What the man didn't know was that she was already in love with him. Both sides of her. A surge of jealousy filled me; knowing that she had touched him, kissed him, held him the same way I was. He looked into her eyes the same way that he was looking into mine. I knew that he wasn't seeing me. He was seeing her golden locks, her taunting sky-colored eyes. I grabbed him, dragging him closer into my kiss. I wanted him to see me. Me: Summer. I had to have him. I needed him. I needed him to need me the same way. I felt his hands move over my clothing, pulling and clawing, wanting me to give him permission. I knew that no matter what I said, he'd take me. He was Lord; he had made that known. I was his captive, and I knew at this moment I was her too.

* * * *

I watched him sleep in my arms. His black hair was disheveled against my skin. His bare skin felt warm and comforting against my own. Was this how it felt to love someone so much? I loved him my entire life, and more. I knew what I had to do. I had to try to remember things that I had been fighting. I had to give him the answers that he deserved; and then maybe he could love me for me.

I wondered who he had just made love to, in his mind. Did he want me, or her? I could feel the tears in my eyes spring to life. My chest pounded, and my heart twisted. The beautiful painting of golden sunshine and his black aura changed into rain. Forest greens with dying leaves and the rain that filled the sky. I wished for a moment that I were a normal girl, lying here with a normal man. One that loved me; one that would wake up and want to hold me close. I felt him stir against me, and I closed my eyes in a panic. I didn't want to be awake in time to be a disappointment. I didn't want to see the regret in his eyes.

I felt him slowly lift himself off of my chest, imagining his dark eyes gazing down at me. I wondered if he knew that I was just faking sleep. What would I say if he said my name? What would I do if he said hers? I felt his fingers touch my cheek ever so gently, and then he pulled away. I could feel the bed shift, and then he was gone. Suddenly, my body felt empty and cold. The only hint of his body was the indent next to mine, and the vague ghost of warmth that was left there. I opened my eyes as I heard my door close, and I felt as if I already knew the answers to all of my questions. He'd forever love her, and I'd always be the vessel that carried her spirit. He had made love to the both of us, in hopes to be nearer to her. I stared up at the ceiling as this knowledge washed over me; a single tear slid down my cheek and onto my pillow.

* * * *

His face was full of sorrow. I wanted to reach out and touch him, but I knew that it wouldn't fix anything. It was a dream, and I was only a spectator. I was watching him say goodbye to Persephone. Her soft golden curls bounced as she climbed up a rocky staircase to the hole that brought her back to the human world. She was her own sunlight, and she was leaving her dark prince to his spirits and darkness. She didn't even look back as she made her escape to the day and the world above. Their words were still echoing around the caves,

"I'll come for you in the fall," his voice had promised. I could see her perfect face give him a short smile and a curt nod. "I love you, my wife."

I felt my stomach churn at his words. How could he not love someone as beautiful as she? She was the kind of girl that ended up in magazines or made movies in my world. Everyone would have wanted her. He lifted her hand to his lips, and he kissed her. She watched him and touched his face for a moment.

"I have to go," she whispered, and then turned toward the stairs. She dashed away from him and his world with each step that she took; away from his love and everything that was made up of him. I watched as she disappeared, and then the hole slowly began to close until there was nothing left but darkness, and then the slight circles of light that guided his boat back through his dark caves. I woke with a jolt and knew that I had to find the answers. I had to bring his aching heart to peace. I would do whatever it took to make him happy again.

Chapter Seventeen

Asphodel Fields was as far as I knew I could go. It was where death and water met and without Charon, I couldn't get any farther. I wanted to find Hecate and get the answers that I had a feeling she harbored. She knew things about Persephone and Demeter that I didn't. More importantly, she knew my mother. Her eyes told me that she held knowledge that Hades wouldn't tell me. I didn't know what had brought me to the fields, but where the spirits were, she would be. I wandered around the dark green and tall browns, hoping that she'd suddenly appear like one of the spirits. I watched as glowing orbs danced around my head and the haunting tree trunks that lurked near the dark shadows of the dead waters. I heard stories of Greek heroes making their way to the Underworld to perform heroic tasks and save their loved ones. I tried to imagine their stony faces, coming to this field, ready to lay their lives before Hades; and he was the kind of man that would take them. A shiver ran up my spine with the thought of him taking lives. He had the power to end life, as Zeus had the power to give life.

"You have nothing to fear, my dear," a soft whisper came from behind me. I turned, catching the crystal eyes of Hecate. She gave me a warm smile and slowly began to walk toward me. She reminded me of a ghost, her steps soft and measured.

"I know why you've come Summer," she whispered, extending a hand toward me. I eyed her pale fingers for a moment and slowly extended mine to take hers.

The touch was electric. Images and sounds filled my mind as our fingers touched. They flashed so quickly that I didn't have the chance to piece them together. She pulled her hand away for a moment with a smile.

"You want to know about your mother," she stated. There wasn't a hint of a question in her voice. Her eyebrow rose, and her lips turned into a tease. "The things that I know are things that Hades does not want you to know."

I wanted to say that I didn't care. I didn't care that she knew things that Hades wanted me to forget. I knew my life at the beach house was over. The days of Art School and my dreams were long gone. There was nothing but the caverns of darkness and the white bed sheets that didn't belong to me.

"I want to know them," I murmured, wanting to grab her hand and insist like a child until she told me the truth. She must have read my facial expression because her lips curved into a larger smile.

"You want to know what happened to Persephone too, don't you?" She began to circle around me; her long, sapphire dress dragged her feet and into the evergreen grass.

"That is why you're here, isn't it? He brought you here to find Persephone." I already knew she had these answers. There was no point in responding. I felt my hopes begin to diminish slowly. Was she really going to tease me with things that I already knew?

"You should know that Persephone did love him," she said, nodding as she eyed me. "And he loved her very much."

"I already know that," I answered, watching her walk in circles around me.

"But Demeter hated him. He was the brother of Persephone's father, her unfaithful lover."

"Zeus," I stated, nodding. I already knew this part of the story. Demeter went to Zeus and begged for him to do something.

"Demeter called on me," she said with a proud smile, glancing up at the gray sky of the caves. Her thoughts seemed far away, in another time, another story.

"She asked me to help save her daughter from the hands of death. She knew that I could come and go from the Underworld as I pleased." She began to pace, swinging her sapphire dress in the slight breeze the waters created. She reminded me of a princess, in a far away land, frolicking for flowers.

"What did you do?" I asked softly, waiting for more of the story.

"Well, I did what she told me to. I met Persephone. I befriended her. I told her about her mother, and how worried she was. Persephone laughed away her mother's worries. She wanted to believe that Hades could love. But everyone knows that Hades cannot love. How can the dark ever become light?" I wanted to open my mouth and tell her that she was wrong, but her face changed. Her eyes became darker, and she shook her head.

"Death can never love something alive. It will only kill it. If you think that Hades could ever love you, you must remove that thought at once. You are here for one purpose for him; to find Persephone. You are only a vessel of a soul to him. That is all."

I felt my head begin to shake. She was wrong. I could see the love in his soul. I could see how badly he wanted to love— needed to be loved. I felt it in the way he held me the night before. The way he kissed me. It was the first time I'd ever made love to anyone, but I knew it was just as real as anything the world above could have offered me.

"You think that you're different from her, but you *are* her. You are one in the same. If you continue this way, you will end up just like her."

"My mother is dead," I snapped. "I don't have a mother plotting to kill me."

"Her mother didn't kill her, Summer. Her mother was just trying to protect her daughter from heartbreak."

"She broke a promise," I said sternly. "Persephone was to be with Hades for only a few months out of the year."

"She didn't want her daughter to be corrupted by his evil thoughts."

"So, what did she do with her then? What did Demeter do to Persephone to hide her away from Hades for all these years?" I knew my voice was getting angrier. I wanted to hold back; compress my anger, and use it to get more answers.

"Persephone was turned mortal," she sighed. "Demeter took her daughter away from the Underworld, and back to her earthly home. She took a liquid drug that she remedied, and gave it to her daughter, and while Persephone went to sleep that night, surrounded by her herbs and flowers, her mother took her peeling knife—"

"Stop. Just stop telling me." I shook my head. I felt disgust and betrayal twist deep inside my bones. I hoped somewhere inside of me; Persephone was listening. Did she remember what it was like to feel the pain in her sleep, and not realize that it was her mother?

"Demeter buried her daughter near the ocean, hoping that the sand and seashells would create a new human form for her daughter to take. And just like she planned, when she was ready, you were created. She called upon me to bring her Persephone's soul, which had been kept carefully hidden in a jar in my home here in the Underworld. I gave the body a soul, and you were born." I felt sick. I could feel the rush of fever and shivers flood my head, and I couldn't find my balance. "I have one more thing to tell you, dearest Summer," she said with a curt grin. "One thing that Hades does know, and has been keeping from you." I knew that I couldn't handle any more truths. I wanted to keep her from saying any more, but I knew that I had no control over her. I could barely stand. "Your mother is alive, and has been following you, and is waiting for you to come home."

My heart gave a dead stop, and I clutched my chest, my nails digging into the frothy silk. "My mother died in the car accident in Greece," I stammered. I already knew what her face was doing. I could feel the smile on her lips. I could feel the pride seeping out of her. No one in the Underworld was who he or she seemed.

"Your mother wants you back home. She wants you to forget this place, and forget him, and come home."

"So she can kill me again?" I felt the words slip through my lips before I could stop them. It was as if the person inside of me was taking control.

"She wants to keep you safe from his darkness. You don't understand what he can do to you, Summer. He can make you lose your soul, forever."

176

"No better than what you did to her," I whispered.
"You took her soul away."

"But I gave it back, and here you are. Without me, you
wouldn't be here." Her tone was full of anger. She wanted
her actions to be justified, but I couldn't play along.

"If my mother wants me so badly," I began. "Then let
her come here. Let her come to the Underworld and face
Hades," I felt my heart begin to weaken, and I knew that I
was about to faint. The pain of the memories flooding my
mind and my body began to paralyze me.

"Don't fight the pain," she whispered, touching my
back gently. I wanted to tear her arms away from me, but I
couldn't move. "Let them come, and then maybe you'll
understand."

I wanted to fight. I wanted to go back to my room,
back to my unkempt sheets where his scent still lingered.
Even if I couldn't have him completely, I could have the
memory of his lips on mine. His hands pressing mine to the
bed and loving me. There hadn't been words, only glances.
I wished that I could keep them forever in my mind, and
relive the moment, over and over again. I wanted him to
take me back to my room, back to the ocean, where I could
paint him, and could fall asleep knowing that he had been
there. He had been there for me, not for her. I fought to see
beyond my watercolors. I fought to see the reality of
everything. Hades had fought to keep me with him, the one
thing that he didn't have the chance to do for her. I had to
do the same. I began to slowly walk away from Hecate,
wanting to reach his kingdom before I couldn't. The pain
became so intense, and I could hear her laughter echo all
around me.

"Let the memories take their course, Summer. You'll have your answers then. Once you release Persephone, everything else will fall into place, and then Demeter will return."

I felt my legs begin to run. My heart was out of control, and I couldn't catch my breath. I had to get to Hades before I collapsed. This is what he had been waiting for. This is what I doubted I could ever do. I tried to test my voice as I reached the large brown doors that led to one of the great meeting halls, but I couldn't gasp anything loud enough for anyone to hear. I ran through the mazes of halls and stairs until I reached my room. I pressed my fingers into my temples again, groaning so loudly that I knew he had to have heard me. I stumbled toward his door, wanting to grab onto the door latch and swing it open. Just as my fingers touched, the door opened, and his dark gaze met mine. First, regret, and then concern.

"I know the truth," I sobbed. "I know what happened to her, to me," I grabbed his cloak and pulled myself into his arms. I wanted to feel his embrace. I wanted to feel the love that was seeping out of me, returned. I wanted to know that everything had been worth it; from the night on the beach to the car accident, to the hospital run-away, to everything else. I felt his arms circle around me and tighten.

"I won't let go," he murmured into my hair. "I won't let you go again."

Chapter Eighteen

My head felt so heavy. Even as I laid on my white bed, full of soaked sheets from my sweaty body, I knew that the only cure was to do as exactly as Hecate said to me as I ran away from her. I had to stop fighting the inevitable. I had to embrace the part of me that belonged to Persephone and finally give her a voice. I saw it in his eyes as he put me into bed, brushing my hair out of my eyes. His eyes begged me to finally give in, and let her breathe again. I heard voices outside of my door, whispering her name, whispering mine. I tried to ignore them and focus on the pain in my head. I built such a tall wall to block her all the things that I didn't want to be inside of me, that trying to tear it down would be difficult.

"This is the only chance I'm giving you to speak," I murmured silently to myself. *"This is your chance to tell me what happened."* I felt the pain in my head begin to throb harder. My pulse leaped from my chest to my temples. The pounding became harder and harder. I gritted my teeth. *"I know you have something to say. You know something that he doesn't, and you have to tell me. You have to show me."* I could feel her twist in my body. Her bones became mine. Her heartbeat joined mine in rhythm. Her breath became my breath. I heard the faint whisper of her voice in the back of mind, but I couldn't make out what she was saying.

"Try again," I managed in between another gasp. *"Show me."* A surge of color awakened behind my eyelids, and the sudden pain peaked before slowly beginning to dwindle away.

179

She stood silently, her golden hair billowing in the slight breeze that I could feel crawl up my skin. I felt like I had left my body, and disappeared into the depths of my mind. She and I finally stood, face to face, her smile warmer than I had imagined. Her sky-colored eyes captured mine, and she extended a hand out toward me.

"We are one in the same, Summer. There is no use pushing me away." Her voice was sweet and soft. Softer than mine. I felt the rush of jealousy flow through my veins. She was perfect, everything that I imagined in my nightmares. "We've come a long way to get here, to this moment," she continued. I watched her slowly walk closer toward me. I extended my hand out to her, knowing there was no use in ignoring her. She was here. She was me. "My mother loved me so much, that she wanted to keep me away from the one man that gave me freedom from her watchful eyes," she whispered, pulling my hand into hers, her fingers grazing over my palm.

"Neither he nor I knew what my mother had planned. She came for me as she usually did, and we rode back to our home in the forest. She gave me warm milk and fruit and slipped me off to bed," her eyes were wild with memories.

I could see them just as she spoke. I could see the warm den, woods-covered with bark and leaves. A little fireplace in the corner of the makeshift home, while Persephone's bed was tucked away between the roots of a tree. Her mother extending her hands with a large wooden cup of white milk, and a slice of bread. The dreams from long ago were beginning to make sense.

"I felt her stab me," I felt the tingle of goosebumps rise on my skin. "I felt the blood pour from my chest, my stomach, my arms, and legs. I felt her tears fall on my face as I died."

I could feel the knife wounds take root in my chest, over and over again. I could feel the warm blood dripping from my fingertips.

"She buried me near the ocean, hoping that the Gods would forgive her, and create a new form for me. I heard the waves roaring over my silent tears until there was nothing left of me," she gazed darkly at me. "Until they took my soul and put it in a jar, where I stayed hidden from everything and everyone that I loved." Her hand tightened around mine. Her eyes were tired and weary, and I wanted to make them bright and happy again. "Until there was you, Summer. You were born to a woman, who was my mother. She took a human husband, and raised you with him."

The flash of my father's face filled my mind, and I missed him. My heart yearned for the only normal part of my life, the only part of my life that wasn't real.

"What my mother forgot was the deal with Hades. She thought that the moment I was dead, I would no longer have to fulfill my deal with him." She looked up at me and gave me a small smile. "But he came for you. He didn't forget about me." Her voice was full of hope. She probably hoped that she'd get a second chance with him. I wished for a moment, looking at her this way, that I could give her that second chance. "And you love him, the same way that I loved him, if not more," she whispered, touching my face with a sad smile. She pulled her hand away, keeping her eyes on her hand. I noticed a golden band around her

181

finger, with a small black stone on it. She slipped it off carefully and pulled at my hand. I shook my head.

"I can't take that. It's yours."

"It's yours now, Summer. He will always be ours in this life, but in your world, you are what he can see and touch and be with. He belongs to you now." She slipped the ring onto my finger and closed my hand. I felt her hand slip away, and she slowly pulled away from me. "And you are his."

Her words echoed in my head. *His*.

"I'm glad you went with him, Summer. You will find that life with him is worth everything. Even facing death." I wanted to grab her hand and tell her to take my body, but I knew that she was slipping away. "You will still have many more things to face, but I hope knowing everything now will give you the strength to persevere."

"I'm sorry I was so mean to you," I whispered, watching her lips curve into a smile. She didn't say anything.

I felt the haze in my head begin to lift, and yet there was no pain. My eyes began to flutter, and they were open. The white room was quiet, and I saw Hades sitting on the edge of the bed, his head in his hands. I slowly sat up, pushing myself up against the pillows. I watched him slowly turn his face to look at me. His eyes were red and bruised with sadness. I wanted to reach out to him and hold him.

"How did you sleep?" he whispered, pushing himself closer to me. I felt his hands on my forehead, checking for a fever that didn't exist.

"I saw her," I whispered, glancing up at him. I lifted my hand and noticed the small band around my finger. I gently pulled on the ring and slipped it into his hand.

"She gave this to you?"

"She was taken from you. She didn't mean to be away for so long," I felt the sadness that I saw on Persephone's face, deep inside of me. I could feel the tears in my eyes spring to life. I watched him play with the golden band in his hand, twirling it around in between his forefinger and thumb. "She loved you," I whispered, gathering all the strength that I could devise, knowing that I was losing him forever as I spoke the words. He loved *her*. He wanted *her*. I'd never be enough.

He wrapped his arms around me, slowly pulling me toward him as if he were unsure if I would go willingly. I felt his cold tears fall on my shoulders, and I returned his embrace. Even if he didn't love me, I had to love him back. His lips were abruptly on mine. I felt him tugging at my clothing, and I wanted to push his hands away.

"I can't," I whispered, shaking my head. He pulled away for a moment, looking at me with confusion in his eyes. "I'm not her," I said slowly. "I'm Summer. I'm the girl that lived next to the ocean, and painted, and went to art school. I'm the girl that misses American food and hates wearing these dresses that you gave me. I'm not Persephone, and she's not coming back." I watched his face clear, and he gave me a curt nod.

"I know who you are," he murmured. "And I know who I made love to before."

I wanted him to whisper my name. I wanted to hear it from his lips that it had been me that he touched and kissed, and not the memory of his wife. I felt his fingers graze over my cheek gently, and his lips curve into a smile.

"Do you know how long it took me to find you, Summer?"

I shook my head, waiting to hear more. I needed to hear what he was about to say.

"I waited years, upon years. It was Hermes. Hermes came to me and told me about your mother. Told me about the human husband she had, and the baby that she'd created. The baby that she had created from the soul of her daughter. No one knew for certain what happened to Persephone's soul, or even if it still existed. I knew. I could feel the heartbeat of Persephone as I slept, thought, dreamed. I knew that one day, Demeter would create a child, and when she did, I would be the one to claim her again," he murmured, glancing up at me with wary eyes. He seemed to be on edge, waiting for me to burst into anger or tears. "When Hermes told me where your mother was living a mortal life with you, I went to your beach house. I watched your father play with you in the sand. Watched your mother watch him, almost as if she were waiting for him to run off with you. I watched you grow, and paint, and play." He was silent for a moment, as he took a deep breath. "I went away for a few years, hoping that maybe I'd move on, or forget. I didn't want your mother to find out that I was watching, waiting for you. And when I came back, you were grown up. You were this beautiful flower that needed tending. Your father was always gone; your mother was always wishing to be with her human husband. And I wished for you. I decided then that I would take you. You had Persephone inside of you. I could feel her voice, her touch, her eyes, everything the moment I looked at you."

"That's all I've been to you," I whispered. "I've been Persephone."

"Not always," he said, shaking his head. "When your parents died, I saw this sadness in you that I knew was yours and yours alone. I wanted to cure you of your sadness. I wanted to tell you that your mother was still alive, but I knew that if you knew the truth, you'd never go with me. You'd choose her, without giving me the chance that you needed."

"You mean, give you the chance that *you* needed," I murmured. He gave a small chuckle and nodded.

"Exactly, the chance I needed," he whispered, giving me a large grin. "It's complicated to tell you my feelings, Summer. To love two women who are the same. One is right in front of me, and the other is deep inside," he sighed, letting out a breath. "I just wanted to know what happened to her. I wanted to know that it wasn't my love that pushed her away. I wanted to know that she loved me back. And before I could even get those answers, I found that *you* loved me. You've loved me even before you knew me."

"I loved an idea. I didn't know who you were," I whispered. I knew that was the truth. I had loved an image— a painting. Not the truth. I saw his smile disappear, and his face became serious.

"As did I," he murmured. "I loved the image that had been painted years and years ago in my head. The way things were, not the way they are now." I watched his eyes

185

glaze with imagined scenes. The way things were; her smile, her laughter, and her love. All hers, not mine.

"I guess I fulfilled my duties to you, then," I whispered, watching his face lift and his eyes meet mine. "I remembered what Persephone could not tell you."

"Yes. I suppose you have." He was silent until he looked away again. "I imagine you miss your home."

I closed my eyes, thinking of the house; the beach, the sand, my paints, and my room. It seemed so distant, and yet so close.

"I can call upon Hermes, and he can take you home tomorrow."

"You don't have to do that," I said, pushing myself toward him. The blankets had twisted themselves around my feet, and I struggled to free myself. He rose from the bed and began to walk toward his door.

"You're going to just let me go? Just like that?" I asked, watching and panicking. I suddenly couldn't find my breath, my pulse fluttering. Where would I go? What would I do? What was I without him? I knew that this was where I truly wanted to stay. *He* was my home.

"Just like that," he murmured as he opened his door. I felt the distance between us grow.

"Wait," I whispered. I watched him turn to look at me, his eyes sad and angry.

"What about my mother? Are you really going to just let me go back to her? After everything, she's done to you and to Persephone and to me? She'll kill me."

He shook his head and sighed. "I'll be sure to tell my brother about her, and what she's done. You won't have to worry about your mother anymore." I watched him disappear behind his black door and heard it silently close.

Chapter Nineteen

A noise in the room woke me from my dreamless sleep. I pushed the twisted white blankets off of my legs and sat up slowly, my focus dashing around the room. His black door was still closed. I crawled from the warm bed and slowly walked toward his door. I wanted him to let me in. I wondered if he was asleep. I could imagine his black hair falling across his face, his white chest rising with each breath. What would he do if I opened the door? I put my hand on the doorknob, slowly turning it, holding my breath. A knock on my own door startled me.

"Summer? Are you in there?" the voice was unfamiliar, but I felt my body gravitating toward the door as if I had done this before. This was something that I had done before in the past, even if it hadn't really been me. I opened the door slightly ajar, unsure of who was waiting behind it. A handsome face met mine, and his lips curved into a smile.

"I think you already know who I am," he said with a chuckle.

I couldn't take my eyes off of the tall God that stood in my doorway. He was dressed in a casual white polo shirt with faded jeans. He looked as normal as any human man that I was used to, but his shoes gave him away. Despite his modern sneakers, on the sides of them, were wings. He was Hermes, messenger of the Gods. His emerald eyes assured me that my guess was right.

"May I come in?" he murmured softly with a kind voice. He glanced over his shoulder for a moment and then looked at me with more urgency in his eyes. I gave an unsure nod and opened the door wider only a little.

"Are you looking for him?" I asked, trying to keep my eyes away from his door. He shook his head as he walked in and toward one of the chairs in the room and sat down.

"I'm here because of him actually," he sighed. "He called on me to take you back home."

I felt my mouth get dry, and my heart began to race as I shook my head. I didn't want that to be true. "I don't want to go home." I heard myself say.

"This feels like déjà vu," he said with a laugh, brushing his fingers through his hair. I felt like he was mentioning the past with Persephone, but I didn't know. I didn't know anything anymore. I did know that I wanted to stay. I wanted to pound on Hades' door and insist that I stay. How could he turn me out like this? "I imagine your mother would like to see you," he said, clearing his throat. "She's been to Mount Olympus, trying to persuade Zeus to go after you. So my taking you away is pretty urgent."

"I don't want to go back to my mother. I don't want anything to do with her, and I don't want Zeus to come after me. I can take care of myself. I came here of my own choosing; that should mean something."

"Well, of course, you did," he said with a genuine smile. "But I'm here to collect you. Your time here in the Underworld is over. I can assure you that many people would be happy to have the option that he is giving you."

"Most people aren't me," I whispered.

I wanted to say that most people didn't love Hades the way that I did. I wanted to be with him, to stay with him forever. He sat in the chair for a moment and sighed.

"I know that this isn't what you want, but this is the way things have to be. At least for now."

"What am I supposed to do when I go back up there? Am I supposed to just pretend that none of this happened? I know the truth, Hermes. I know the truth about Demeter, and Persephone and what really happened. You can't expect me to go back to her, not like this. What if she kills me too?"

He slowly shook his head and crossed his arms over his chest.

"She won't. She can't. Everyone is looking for you and her right now. If she were to make a move like that, she'd wait until the attentions were focused on someone else. By then, I'm sure the Lord will have some sort of plan organized to keep you safe."

I felt the trickle of fear that I hadn't ever felt for my mother. She could kill me. She could do all sorts of things to me that no one would ever know about, except him. He was my only ally. And right now, he didn't want me.

"Please don't take me away, Hermes. Please. I'm begging you." I felt the tears spring to life, and I knew that I wouldn't be able to control them. I needed more time; needed the time to show him how I needed him. "I just want to stay with him. I love him," I whispered. "I'm old enough to make decisions for myself. This is the twenty-first century after all."

"I can't do anything, my dear. My hands are tied. I have orders, and I have to obey them." He said as he slowly rose from the chair. "If it were up to me," he began. "I'd help you stay. But I can't."

I glanced back at the black door, feeling myself move toward it. I felt my hands on the doorknob, twisting and my body submerging into the darkness. It smelled of must and sea salt, and something damp. Something non-human. Death. In the corner, closest to the door was an arrangement of black candlesticks, and the faint glint of light. There were shadows that painted the walls, and then something bright. Something different. A painting. *My* painting.

"Summer," I heard Hermes hiss at me. I turned around and saw his disgruntled face.

"You're going to wake him."

"Good," I said loudly, turning toward the shadow form of his bed, and what I imagined was his white, solid body.

I felt my legs carry me to the black bed, and I stood, gazing over him. I knew he was awake. I knew he could see me, hear my breath hitch. I didn't wait to hear him say my name.

"Why?" My breath was soft, and I saw him lean up on his elbows, staring at me. I heard him sigh, hesitating to answer.

"We both said it ourselves, Summer. We both loved an image. It's not who we are."

"Why are you turning me over to her now?" I hoped he heard the betrayal in my voice. I felt like a prisoner all over again.

"I thought you *wanted* to go home," he whispered, leaning back on the bed. I climbed on the starch blankets and leaned over his dark form.

"I might have before, but I want to stay here now," I murmured.

"It's impossible," he grumbled. "I have orders to hand you back to your mother from my brother."

"I belong to you. Don't I have to stay here or something, forever? I'm mortal after all. I can't just leave." I asked, searching for any reason to stay. There had to be.

"Hermes will be able to get you out, and as long as you have my approval, you can leave unscathed. Anyone can leave the Underworld with my approval." His voice was stern. There was nothing else. This was it. There was no point in trying to fight with fate when he controlled everything.

"Don't you see what I'm trying to do? I'm trying to stay with you. Why won't you let me?" I could feel the air rush out of my lungs. My pleas were going unheard. I could tell by the dark look in his eyes.

"Do you want me to say the words, Summer? Do I really have to tell you things that are only going to make this worse?"

"What's the worst you can say to me now? Don't you want me? I already can see that." I pushed myself off the bed, hoping for a moment that he'd grab my arm, tell me to stay. I felt my rage seep through my body and out my fingertips the longer he didn't. If I had a brush and canvas, I could see the red flowing like blood. The blood of hurt and betrayal. I turned around, walking back to Hermes' form in the doorway. "Take me home," I whispered as I brushed past him. "I've had enough of this nightmare."

I walked out hearing Hermes closing the black door behind me, leaving the death prince to his eternal darkness.

Chapter Twenty

The raindrops on the windshield were steady and constant. I glanced over my shoulder at Hermes, who was driving quietly and quickly, zigzagging in and between the other cars. His method of getting me back to Athens was quicker than the path that Hades had taken before in the other direction. We were already hours ahead of schedule. The little town of Gythion had come and gone, and the long road to Athens was ahead of us.

"You're a quiet, little one," Hermes murmured, glancing at me for a moment. I felt my shoulders rise and fall, and I let out a quiet sigh. I was fighting sleep, tooth, and nail. I knew that if I fell asleep, I would feel his hands on me, his lips on my neck. I would lose myself in the painting that I had created of him and I together. I couldn't let myself cry. I would not. Crying would do nothing for our situation. It wouldn't bring him back, and it wouldn't bring me closer to him. It was over.

"You shouldn't bother thinking of him, Summer. He's no good. There's a reason why his brother put him down there."

"You shouldn't talk about him like that," I whispered. I felt the air on my arms rise, and I brushed my hand over my goosebumps.

"You deserve better, Summer. I think we both know that."

"Can we just not talk about this?" I snapped, turning my body toward the car door and resting my head against the side window.

"We'll be in Athens in about an hour. From there, the airport, and you'll be back in America."

"I don't care, Hermes. I hate to be the brat, but I just don't care anymore."

Hermes pursed his lips for a moment and then leaned his fingers toward the radio dials, turning on the soft hum of classical music through the speakers. I felt my eyes get heavier and heavier, and I could see the fresh images of Hades. His face, his eyes, and his words, as I'd glance up at the ceilings of the hotel rooms, where we stayed. His touch and his smile. The bathtub and the escape from the hospital. It all seemed like it had happened years ago, and it only happened weeks ago.

"What is my mom—I mean, what is Demeter like?" I murmured, quietly. Hermes turned his head for a moment, licking his bottom lip and then turned back to the wheel.

"Your mother?"

"She's Demeter, right?" I asked slowly, waiting patiently for his answer. Hermes slowly nodded.

"Yes, she's Demeter."

"Is she going to kill me… again?" My last word made his eyebrows rise.

"So you know what happened to Persephone then?"

"Doesn't everyone know?" I asked, more surprised and alarmed. Could it have been that everyone knew, but Hades?

"Not everyone. It's not something that Demeter or Zeus like to share." Hermes said, lifting a corner of his lips up in a smile.

"Does she plan to do something like that to me?" I asked, trying to remember my mother's face. Her laughter, her voice, her touch on my back. The woman that had been my mother for most of my life had somehow become disfigured and deformed in my mind into a darker, stranger-like being. She was no longer my mortal mother.

"If she has those plans, then only one person knows them. And that's herself," he said, letting out a sigh. I looked down at my hands. I had never felt so alone and isolated.

The hour went by in a flash, and the buildings began to grow larger and taller, and the shuffle of traffic became thicker and slower. Hermes tried to speed past as many cars as he could until he finally reached the local Holiday Inn that had been arranged for us to stay in for the night.

"Do not judge, complain or ridicule," he said as he dragged our bags into the tiny room.

I didn't say a word until I saw the white, clean shower. "You did well," I said with a smile as I came out of the bathroom in a pair of my pajamas and a white towel wrapped around my head.

"Good," he said with a laugh, clicking the TV channels with the black remote in his hand. The tacky flower comforter made me feel lost in the queen bed, and I wished silently for the white sheets back in my old room, down in the Underworld. I tried to press the image out of my head. That part of my life was over, forever. I had to forget about him and everything that happened. My future was my mother, and college, and hopefully some kind of normalcy that I hadn't ever allowed myself to have. This could be my new beginning. I saw my bag of paints and brushes, and the clean white sheets of paper that had been packed beside it.

"Do you mind if I go out on the balcony and paint?" I asked Hermes as I slowly bent over, picking up the bag.

"Just as long as you promise not to go running off."

"Where can I go?" I laughed.

"True," he said with a shrug. "But I've heard that heights weren't an issue with you once before."

"There's a difference," I sighed, knowing that he was talking about my attempted escapes with Hades. "The difference is I'm going home now." I wanted the words to mean something. I wanted to feel inside that home was a place I *wanted* to go. But the home that I created for myself was in the other direction. I was drawing farther and farther away from where I wanted to be. I slipped behind the glass door that led into nighttime and glittering stars, and I dipped my paintbrushes into the old paints from my home on the beach. I could hear the honking of horns, and I could see the distant lights from other homes, and hotels. This place was so foreign to me. The sounds were more alarming and annoying, and all I wanted was the silent darkness of the corridors of the Underworld.

I felt my fingers take the brushes and paint long, curvy black lines that became walls, doors and faces that I had met and seen. I wanted to look out and see my ocean again and see the dark figure moving closer and closer to me on the beach. I wanted to hear his whispered promises of taking me away, loving me and keeping me forever. I wanted to follow him back into the place that was ours, and I wanted to be enough. I wanted to be enough for him.

"How's the painting coming?" I jumped at the sound of Hermes' voice, and I gave him a curt smile. I didn't want him to know the truth. I didn't want him to see into my eyes and know what I was really seeing and feeling.

"Good, I suppose."

"Good. It's getting late. You should probably wrap up what you're doing and come in. You're going to have a long day tomorrow." I gave him a small nod and slowly stood up from the chair and began to pack up my brushes and paints. I could feel the dread in my stomach crease and curl into my bones, and it made it harder for me to move back into the hotel room.

"You know," he began. "You said you didn't want to talk about it, but I'm sure this is hard for him too."

I didn't reply to his comment. I wanted that to be true, but I knew that Hades was happy to get rid of me. I may have wanted him to be everything to me, but I knew that I couldn't be the one thing that he wanted the most. I walked past Hermes lost in thought as I trailed myself to the bathroom to brush my teeth.

I pulled myself into one of the single beds in the room after I emerged from the bathroom, and ignored the light buzzing sound coming from the TV. I saw Hermes still wide awake, stretched out on his bed, one arm under his head as he flipped the channels, all humming of foreign languages. I tried to hide under the covers and close my eyes. Maybe I would wake up in the Underworld, and I'd be given a second chance. Or even wake up in Rhode Island and all of this would be an ironic dream. I'd stop reading and daydreaming about the Greek Gods. I promised myself that I'd never paint his face again, as I finally let myself fall into a deep sleep.

Chapter Twenty-One

The air around me was buzzing in my ears. It seemed all I could hear was the static from the television and the sound of coffee being poured into heat-resistant cups. I felt like I could still sleep for hours on end. My body wasn't used to the mortal world, and I felt crazy for thinking that way. I could blame it on the past few weeks, going back and forth from real life to the life that had been created from paintings and mythical stories. I watched the collection of people sitting around us at different tables, eating their morning bagels and bowls of cornmeal with boiling milk on top. The tourists had their maps set out over their tables, reading and choosing places to go for the day. I watched Hermes brush his hair out of his face and tug his white t-shirt down over his jeans as he took a sip from his coffee.

"Are you sure you only want a muffin?" he asked as he sat down across from me. "It is a free breakfast after all."

I gave him a small smile and nodded. "I'm not really a breakfast or morning person," I explained and shrugged as I put my once-bitten-into-muffin down on the table. At least, I had hot coffee, and I hoped it would do the trick in waking me up. Hermes pushed me out of bed earlier, telling me that we had a very strict schedule to keep to for the day; meeting my mother and flying back home to the United States. Coffee was the only option to get me completely functioning.

"I got a call from your mother this morning," he said glancing at me as if he wasn't sure how I would take the news. "She's in Athens, and she said she'd meet us here at the hotel."

"When?" I asked, feeling my body jolt awake. I guess I just needed a good scare. My defense mechanisms hummed to life.

"In the next half hour or so." He glanced at his watch and then back up to me. "Is that alright?"

"What am I supposed to say to her?" I knew that I looked helpless. I felt helpless. My mother, the woman who had not only killed her daughter once but might kill again, the woman who faked her own death, was coming for me. The woman I hadn't seen since the day I thought she died. So much had happened to me since then.

"I know that you're panicking right now, kid. And that's okay. Just take a deep breath. Take a sip of your coffee," he comforted the best he could, pushing the hot cup closer to me. I lifted the warm Styrofoam to my lips and tried to focus on the heat going down my throat and into my body. The warmth became the burning of sand and salt on open wounds and the rumble of ocean water around my ears. All I wanted was to go back to Hades. The yearning in my chest was crushing, and I felt my eyes water.

"Summer, you okay?" I heard Hermes' voice, and I opened my eyes, startled.

"Yeah," I whispered, pushing the cup away from me. "I think I might go back upstairs until she gets here." I felt his hand on my back, and before I knew it, he was leading me back to the elevator where we rode to the top floor and back into our tiny, shared room.

I fell onto my unmade bed, and pressed my face into the bleached sheets, hoping that I could sleep the minutes away until she was here.

"Summer," I felt a warm hand on my back, and I opened my eyes, glancing at the clock and then back up at Hermes. An hour had already passed. My stomach dropped, and I held my breath. "She's here. She's coming up to the room. You might want to get up and comb your hair."

I rolled my eyes, ignoring his suggestion, and patted my bed hair down. I didn't care what I looked like to her. I knew that all the Gods and Goddesses were perfect, and I was not one of them. And that was the reason why I was no longer wanted in the Underworld.

The knock on our cream-colored door startled me more than it should have and I held my breath. Hermes walked toward the door, opening it, and allowing the familiar voice into our room. A tall, brown haired woman came into my view, one that was familiar and yet so foreign. She looked like she belonged on the cover of some European fashion magazine. She didn't look like the woman who had picked me up at college or had forced me to pack up all our belongings and move to Greece. She was a woman of power and wealth and something that I could never be.

"Summer," she sighed with a smile and extended her arms out to me.

I didn't move. I couldn't move. I felt her cold arms wrap around me and hold me close to her rose-scented shoulders. She wasn't my mother, no matter how much I wanted her to be. She was a murderer. She was the reason I was here, and not with him. I tried to force the thought out of my head. He didn't want me. He didn't want the *other* girl. He wanted the real deal. I could never be Persephone, and all because of this woman in front of me.

"Look at you," she said with a larger smile. "You look like you've been to hell and back." She laughed and looked at Hermes. "I suppose she has, hasn't she?" She glanced back to me, and I felt the heat of anger grow in my fists, and I squeezed them harder. "Aren't you happy to see me, darling? Aren't you glad to know that one of your parents is still alive?"

I wanted to reply with the truth. Would it be so terrible if I had said that I wasn't glad? That I wished that she were dead? That I wished that the man who had been my father were alive instead? That I wanted to be with anyone but her right now? *He doesn't want you. He doesn't want you, Summer.*

"Yeah," I whispered softly, letting the lie fill the room.

I knew Hermes heard the acid in my voice. He glanced at me, wanting me to try to make things work better than I was.

"Now you can move back home, and you can pursue your painting school again. You can do anything you want."

"I don't want to paint anymore," I said softly, knowing that it was true. I knew that I couldn't paint anything other than Hades and the memories that we recently created. Painting them would only put my life in danger, and I could find something better to do with my time. Maybe I could go away to college and study history, or writing, or anything else but art.

"Alright then," she said with a smile and sat down on the edge of Hermes' bed. "Well, there are other things you can do. Better things."

I noticed a brown clay jar, sitting on the table in front of me. That hadn't been there before. I glanced at the woman beside me: Demeter, not my mother, and I knew what jar that was. What it meant; the warning behind it. She would trap me in the jar again, pushing my soul into another body form. All of this would become just a distant memory again, until whoever the future me would be realized who they were. Would they remember me? The 'Summer' girl who had been stolen away? Would Hades come for her too? Or would he give up, and finally move on. Forget about me and whoever else came after me. He knew his answer about Persephone. She was dead, and I would be too. Someday.

"I have tickets to go home for us, Summer," she said with a firm face. "We'll be getting back to our home in no time, and we can talk about everything that happened." Her hands grabbed mine, and I pushed them away. I couldn't bear the feeling of her cold hands on mine.

"There is nothing to talk about," I said, finishing the conversation. I didn't want to talk about Hades, or the Underworld or what had happened to me. I was better off living in the fantasy than facing what would and could happen to me.

"I'm sure there are a lot of questions you have for me, darling."

"Don't call me darling," I snapped. "I'm no one's darling."

I saw my mother's face change into something darker, and more evil. She was angry and yet so was I. She was the worst betrayal yet.

"If *he* told you to act like this toward me, you better think twice, *sweetheart.*"

I knew that I had better stop what I was doing. If I wanted to live, to go home, and get away on my own time, I had better just stop. I nodded, and gave her a small smile, faking it as well as I could.

"I'm sorry, mother," I whispered. "I'm just tired." I tried to manage out an excuse, hoping she would believe me.

I saw Hermes let out a breath of air. Everything could fall apart, even before it began if I wasn't careful with what I said. I knew I had a role to play, and I had to set my anger aside, at least until I got home. From there, I could plan some sort of run-away. I knew in the pit of my stomach, if I ran, I'd always be on the run. I'd always be alone.

"The most important thing I have to ask you, Summer, is such a simple question, though if you answer wrongly, you will face many consequences," she said, her gaze flicking to Hermes first, and then me. I knew what she was going to ask. She wanted to make sure the Lord of Death didn't have any bonds over her spring child.

"Have you eaten anything from the Underworld?" This was my chance to lie and say yes and perhaps return to him. Maybe then he'd keep me, fight for me. This couldn't be it. There was something in my heart that was refusing my grim reality. Even if she decided to kill me, wouldn't I just go back to the Underworld? Wouldn't Hades be able to do something to save my soul, and keep me with him?

"No," I said shaking my head.

"There now, Demeter," Hermes began. "Your daughter is your own again. You can take her home and know that she is free from Hades forever."

Something in her eyes suggested that she didn't believe his words, nor mine. She was still very suspicious.

Hermes gathered my things, whatever I had left from my long journey, and carted it to the door. I felt my mother's arms around my shoulders as her hands petted my hair, and her lips met my forehead.

"Everything will be alright, my darling. We'll go home, and we can figure everything else later."

Just before Hermes closed the car outside of the hotel a few minutes later, Hermes held me.

"Stay strong, kid," he murmured and pulled me out of the hug to look at me. "I have on good authority that everything will be alright with her."

I gave him a curt nod as I pushed myself out of his arms and into the car where my mother was waiting. I had a long flight back to the States with her, and I wasn't even sure what to say. I knew what not to say; nothing that had to do with Hades.

"Ready to go home?" she asked as Hermes shut the door, and I gave her a silent nod.

Chapter Twenty-Two

I tossed back and forth in my old bed. I couldn't get to sleep. This was the one place I had been longing for, for so long, and now that I was back, it felt so foreign. I could hear the faint rumble of ocean waves, and my room still smelled of paints and oils, just the way it had when I had left it. It was empty; the walls were still bare. I tried to curl myself into the comforter, hoping that something would finally put me to sleep, but nothing. I suddenly wished for a bathtub. I knew that I could take my pillows and blankets in the tub and sleep much better there than I was in this bed, but I wasn't back in our hotel room with the colorful lights. I was here, at home. Back in America, with my mother.

I glanced at the red alarm clock on the bed table and wanted to curse. It was almost four in the morning. I tried to let my eyes close and allow sleep to take over my body, but it seemed like nothing was working. My mind was back under the ground with the faceless shadows, Thanatos, Hecate and him. I could imagine Thanatos' face, full of victory and amusement. He had won. His master had gotten rid of me. If I could see him again, I was sure I'd punch him in the face. I didn't care if he had stronger powers than me. I could feel the imaginary me, peeling back the white sheets from my old bed in the palace and opening his black door, walking to him slowly. Seeing him sitting on the edge of his deathbed, and watching me as I walked closer to him. There wouldn't be any more talk of my mother, or Persephone. There would just be us. Our hands would connect, fingers grazing over skin and cloth and lips. He

would whisper my name and hold me close, the way I
wanted him to.

"I love you, Summer." The dark whisper startled me,
waking me from the light sleep I had put myself in. The
room was bright, and I could hear my mother doing
something in the hallway. I wasn't sure if she was cleaning
or bringing in boxes, but I knew she was trying to bring our
old lives back into the house, minus the man who called
himself my father.

I pushed myself from the bed, tugging on some jeans
and a fresh shirt from the pile of clothes in the corner of my
room. I really needed to get some clean clothes. I leaned
over, trying to look for a different shirt or anything else to
wear, and found a folded pile of silk and softness and knew
it had to be one of the dresses that Hades had given to me. I
stared at it for a moment, not knowing if I should throw it
away, or lift it up to my nose and see if I could smell him.
A knock on the door startled me, and I dropped the fabric
into the pile of clean and dirty clothes before I opened the
door slowly. My mother's smiling face greeted me.

"Glad you're awake. I was going to ask you if wanted
to grab something to eat," she said with a smile, and I
slowly shook my head.

"I'm not really hungry," I began. She cut me off and
opened my door a little more.

"Nonsense. The last time you ate was at the hotel. You
refused dinner. You've got to be hungry."

I shook my head, wanting to protest when she came
into my room. I hadn't eaten when we arrived home
because I knew she'd want to stop for something fast along
the way back to the house, and my stomach was nowhere

near willing to eat her fried foods. I stopped her at the entrance to my room, and stood in front of the pile of clothes, in hopes that she wouldn't see the silk clothing or the other things from my travels. I knew the moment she was out of sight; I'd have to find a place to hide them.

"Summer, darling, I want you to eat," she said as she cupped my cheek, paying more attention to what I hoped were the dark circles under my eyes and perhaps how thin I had become from the long journey. I knew to get her away from me, I'd have to agree, and she'd finally leave me alone to find something to cook, or heat up, or go get.

"Alright, Mother." I whispered the words and watched as her concerned face turned into a pleasant smile and she seemed happy with my change of mind.

"Good then," she said and turned around, heading for the staircase. "I'll go out and get us something to eat. You take a shower and get clean."

I wasn't used to her orders. I didn't remember her being so bossy about small things like showers and eating. Or maybe it was just that I was so used to Hades being the one that ordered me around; when I could change, when we'd eat when we'd sleep.

She smiled at me one last time before she descended the stairs, and slipped out of the house. I turned back to my room, noticing a box in the corner, near my windows. I pulled it open, not sure what could be inside. I thought that mostly everything that I had boxed up had been shipped to Greece, and I could only imagine what happened to our belongings after I had gone to claim my clothes and paints.

I pushed away the packing peanuts and dug into the box until my hand touched something round and hard, and smooth. I gripped it tightly and gently pulled it out of the packing peanuts. In my hands was the jar I had seen in my dreams. The very jar that Persephone showed me when she told me her tragic story. I turned it gently in my hands; looking at the delicate design; the small flowers and the tiny seeds from what looked like could be a pomegranate. This had to be the jar that Demeter put her daughter in. The only question was what was it doing in my room? I didn't want Demeter, my mother, to see what I had unearthed from her box of secrets. All I could think of was that I had to free her. I had to open this jar and free myself, free the spirit of who I was in another time, and maybe then, I'd have the chance to move on. Maybe then I could finally be just Summer. Just me.

I quickly stood up, pushing my door open, and ran down the stairs to the kitchen. The table was set for a meal; my mother even had some lilies in a vase. It was so odd to see my mother taking enough time to put flowers on the table. It wasn't something that she used to do. I ignored them, pushing myself past the crusty sink and to the paint-chipped door. I pulled it open, escaping to the back patio and finally to the ocean. It was the way that I remembered it; the way I knew it would always be.

I stood in front of the waves for a short while, taking in the salty air, the sand between my toes and the slight chill that ran down my spine as the waves gently lapped near my feet. Finally, I looked down at the jar in my hands and knew this was going to be the only chance I had to do this. I had to free Persephone, if not myself. And maybe even free Hades in the process. Free him from the torment of a lost wife.

I tried to pry the top with my fingers, but it seemed to be firmly sealed. There was no end or beginning to the lid, even though I could faintly feel the grooves where the opening should have been. I became desperate. I glanced back at the patio and noticed some fairly large stones near our home. I ran back to the yard and picked one up in my hand. I looked at the rock, weighing it with my hands. The weight of freedom was heavy. I dropped the rock on the jar, attempting to smash it open, but the rock seemed to bounce right back into my hand. I set the jar down on the patio stones and tried to slam the rock again and again against the top of the jar. I had to free her. *Free her. Free her. Free Me. Free…him…*

"What are you doing?" My mother's voice startled me. I hadn't realized I had been out there longer than five minutes. I quickly glanced down at the jar and then at my mother. I couldn't hide it from my face. She knew exactly what I was doing. My throat closed, the inside of my mouth going dry.

"Do you honestly think that's going to work?" She seemed to be almost scoffing me. I quickly picked up the jar and held it close to my chest. "Don't you think I thought about someone trying to break that open?" She gestured to the jar angrily.

I didn't know what to say. I must have known she would have done something to make it impossible. It was Demeter after all, and she was trying to keep her daughter, me, or Persephone, or whoever we were together, in her control. I watched her walk toward me, reaching her hand out for the jar.

"Give it to me." She sneered, and I shook my head quickly, shoving the jar behind my back. The sand was scratching against my toes. My mother, Demeter, didn't stop until she was standing right in front of me. She could have easily wrapped her arms around me and grabbed the jar from behind my back. "You will give it to me, Summer," She said a bit more sternly. I eyed her.

"What if I don't?"

"You think this is a game? You think that I'll just let you keep it? It's not a toy."

"I know it's not. It's me."

"You can't even begin to understand—"

I quickly shook my head, cutting off my mother. "No, it's you who doesn't understand." I backed away a bit more. "You tried to separate them, us, Persephone and Hades, me and him. You tried so hard, and yet, you failed."

"I didn't fail," she barked out laughter, shaking her head, her hands falling down at her sides. "No, I think I walked away with my daughter."

"You walked away with a dead daughter. You walked away as a murderer."

"You're right here. You are my daughter." She said, reaching out for the jar again. "Give me the jar, Summer."

"Why can't you just admit that you killed her? You trapped her, and killed her, and then stole all her memories, and made me. How do you think I feel?"

Demeter shook her head, raising her hand to silence me. "How do you think I feel, doing this again? Do you think I want to hurt you, Summer? You're my darling baby. My second chance. My only chance, and now you've seen him. Now things are different. Things can never be the way they were."

"It all makes sense now," I whispered. "The reasons why you didn't like my fascination with him. Why you tried to get me to be around people more often." She looked at me as if she had nothing to deny. All of it was true.

"And my father?" I questioned her a bit more angrily. "The one piece of my life that was normal and you took him away from me?" I watched her face grow serious and thoughtful for a moment and then she was angry again. Her eyes were flames that were ready to lick my skin and scald me.

"You were never supposed to know any of this, Summer. You were supposed to grow up like every other human, and live, and then die. And then that would be the end. I would finally let you and her go."

"I really doubt that," I said a bit too harshly. After a long moment of nothing but the sounds of the waves, she sighed, dropping her hand to her side.

"What do you think he's going to do for you? He has nothing to offer you. He can't give you a normal life like I can." she said, trying to find reasons for me to stay with her; desperate pleas from a desperate mother. It was easier to ignore her, remembering that she really wasn't my mother anymore.

"I don't expect anything from you," I whispered. "It's over."

"Exactly," she said a bit happier. "It's over. You're home, and we can start over again."

"I can't just forget about this," I snapped. I brought the jar in front of me, holding it toward her. "There is a dead

211

girl, a dead form of me, in my hands right now. I can't just ignore that this ever happened. You have killed a piece of me that my memory wants to know— wants to remember so badly. And I will know her," I promised.

She stared at the jar for a moment and then at me, an almost apologetic look crossing her face.

"I want you to let me go," I finally said, gesturing to the jar and the ocean. "Let me go. Break this, and let it go. You can't keep us trapped forever."

I watched my mother look at the jar and then me again, her eyes darting between the alive and dead daughter; the both of us the same, and then something else crossed her eyes. Something darker that I hadn't seen before. I suddenly felt her hand around my wrist, and she grabbed the jar from my hand and tugged me behind her towards the waves. I knew what was going to happen. I knew I was going to die, just like Persephone. She would push me into the water, and somehow take my soul and trap it with Persephone's soul, and then I too would become only a memory to Hades.

"I'll set you free," she whispered over and over again, hastily. I knew not to fight her. The battle was over, and she would win again.

Chapter Twenty-Three

I was ready to give up. I watched as my mother, no, not my mother, Demeter, violently dragged me towards the ocean waves. I knew this was the end. It was crazy to think that all of this had started right here, on the beach. Right here, in the ocean, where he had come so quietly, so dark, and now I was going to die right here in these waves, quietly. She tugged on my hand until we reached the breach of ocean and sand, and she stood, letting out a breath of salty wind and droplets of the sea that had landed on her lips. She turned toward me, looking at me with her sad, now-crazed eyes, and shook her head.

"It could have been different for you, Summer. He just had to come and ruin it for the both of us."

I shook my head, knowing that if there was one thing he had done, he had opened my eyes to the truth. She must have seen the disagreement on my face because she quickly let go of my hands and pushed me into the waves, where I landed on the rough sand and shells with my palms. I let out a shriek of pain as she grabbed me by my hand and pushed me deeper into the water, until my body was completely submerged, except for my face. She pushed the jar into the water and slowly began to open the lid. I could see a faint golden light coming from the inside of it; the hum of something sweet and golden traveled in the water to my ears. At first, I began to panic and then I heard my name. I heard Persephone calling for me. She was alive in my mind again, alive in every sense of the word.

I saw flashes of the past, the golden sun, and dancing in wide green fields with delicate flowers under my toes. A red flower, the ground opening up from under me, and then darkness. Death. Hades. Present, my mother, my father and the beach, the smell of my oil paints, the feel of the brush in my hand, paper, and college and then there was something in the distance. Him, watching me from the beach. Him, on my walls, in my mind, in my paintings. The future. It was him.

"Summer…" the distant voice grew louder in my ears as the golden light seemed to envelop me in the water. I couldn't feel my mother's hands on my back anymore. The light filled me; gave me a strength I never knew I had. I could feel myself pulling away from my mother's grasp, mentally and physically. She and I would no longer be connected. We would no longer be mother and daughter. It had to just be Summer. Just Summer. *Just Summer…Just Summer…*

"This is over," I could hear Demeter hiss behind me. "Hades will never have you again…"

I could feel the anger inside of me grow. It grew beyond the flashes of fields and flowers and laughter, beyond the darkness and ghosts, beyond the ocean and the end. It was a fire that grew and burnt, until suddenly, I felt my own strength pushing against her. I slammed her back into the water and stood up. She still had the jar in her hands, and I jumped on her. I tried to grab it from her claws, but she resisted, screaming in my ears, scratching my skin, pushing me away. I saw her take a knife from her pocket and point it towards me.

"I won't let you win, Summer," she snarled, shaking her head with a small laugh. "You won't win." I watched as she slowly walked toward me, the water just below her knees. I stood frozen; waiting.

"Summer..." The voice whispered again, *"Run..."* I didn't need to be told twice. I raced out of the water, pushing past Demeter as she tried to grab me. I heard her chasing after me, shouting my name as I left her behind. I heard her screaming as I ran into the house until I slammed into the kitchen table. I saw the car keys lying there, and I grabbed them. I didn't look back. I pushed through the living room and out the front door. I got into our car, and backed out, leaving my screaming mother and my house behind. I turned the car onto Ocean Road and drove north as fast as I could. I didn't pay attention to the houses around me, or the woods. I could feel tears stir in my eyes, and I tried to hold them back. I tried to think of something else, anything else. I couldn't cry. I needed to focus on getting away. My clothes were clinging to me. I was getting the seats all wet. I wished that I still had a suitcase of clothes. It would make hiding out so much easier.

I stopped the car at "Aunt Carrie's." It was a local restaurant that my father would indulge me with once in a while. I knew I couldn't stay long. I had only minutes. I lowered my head to the steering wheel and let out a soft cry. I had nowhere to go. I had no one to turn to. I had no money, no clothes, and a car with half a tank of gas. I could probably make it to another town, get a few hours away, but eventually, I'd run out of gas, and then, I'd be stuck. I'd be alone. I had failed at freeing Persephone. I had failed at freeing myself from Demeter. I could feel the hot tears fall down my cheeks, and I wrapped my arms around myself, trying to stop.

"Summer," I said to myself. "Stop it. Stop it. You have to keep going. You have to keep driving. You have to…" Find him. Find Hades. The thought flashed in my mind. His smile, his eyes, the feel of his hand on mine. His voice, his laughter. My heart yearned for him. Yet, I knew that I couldn't be with him. There was no winning in this battle with her. It was down to being on the run forever from my mother, or turning around and facing her, and finishing this, and possibly dying. I jumped when I heard a knock on my window. I was too afraid to lift my head. It could be my mother. It most likely was. I heard the knocking again, this time on my side of the window. I buried my head in my hands, trying to stop crying. I was going to die here; right here in the parking lot and no one was going to help me.

"Summer." The soft tone of his voice echoed around me, and I slowly lifted my head to see Hades staring at me. A rush of emotions flew through my system. At first, I wanted to let myself cry more. I wanted to open the door and throw myself at him. I wanted to slap him and yell at him for letting me go; letting me go back with Demeter. He had known this was going to happen. He had known that Demeter would have found out, and possibly would have tried to take me out the same way she had killed Persephone.

He tapped the window again and mouthed, "Open your door." I opened the door slowly, unlatching the handle and watched as he opened the door the rest of the way. I was in disbelief. Was he really here? His face was solemn, and his dark hair hung in his face. He looked so perfect. I wanted to touch his face and hold it to mine, kiss him, and never let go. What was I saying? This man let *me* go. This man caused all this trouble in my life. I wasn't about to just proclaim my love and act like nothing had happened between us. I bit my lip, holding back the range of emotions as I watched him gesture for me to get out of the driver's seat.

"Let me drive," he murmured.

"Where are we going?" I asked as I crawled into the passenger seat. He looked at me with his dark eyes and shrugged.

"That's up to you." He glanced ahead, watched the passing cars drive by us and then he turned to look at me. "I'm just here."

"Why are you here?" I whispered, quickly looking away from him.

I heard him take a breath, and slowly let it out. In and out. I played with the elastic hair band around my wrist. I felt like a schoolgirl; a young, stupid teenager completely infatuated. I was better than this. I never let myself feel this way before. Someone who wasn't in my situation would say I had Stockholm Syndrome or something, and maybe they'd be right. Maybe what I was feeling was all from being harassed, stolen and then bossed around. I didn't love him for treating me that way. I didn't love that he could be a total jerk; that he could just take me away from everything that I owned and loved; he could chase me around the world, in cities, towns, fields and tell me what to do and then banish me when I finally did what he wanted me to do. I hated it all. I glanced at him and bit my bottom lip harder. But I *did* love this; the look of confusion and uncertainty, the nights of staring at the dim red light in the hotel rooms while he talked to me, the feel of his arms around me, the look he had on his face every morning when I woke up. It wasn't perfect, but it was real. We were by no means perfect people, but we were real. All of this was real.

"I came back to help you."

"I don't need—"

"Yes you do, you stubborn girl. Did you just forget who you were running from?" he snapped, glaring at me. I shook my head and sighed. "I came back for you, whether you decide to go back to your mother or if you want to run," he explained and turned the key in the ignition. "You just say where and I'll drive."

"She's going to kill me," I said slowly. "She's going to kill me and then you, and what good will that do the both of us?" I heard Hades laugh a little. An eerie laugh.

"She can't kill me. I'm much older and obviously much wiser…" he started. "She doesn't stand a chance against me."

"So you just want me to stroll back into my house, bait myself, and hope that you come in after me?" I didn't know if I should feel outraged or not surprised. I certainly wasn't surprised. Hades shook his head and gave me an amused look.

"You really haven't changed at all. Still jumping to conclusions." I could hear the humor in his voice, and he was already making me angry. "You get to make the decisions, now, Summer. You get to decide if you want to see her again and face her, or not. You get to decide how it happens. I'm just here. I told you."

I didn't show my surprise. I didn't want to look like I had expected the worst from him. I was used to expecting the worst. "And what if she tries to kill me, then what?"

"Then I suppose we fight this together."

"Why else did you come back?" I asked again, and I heard him let out a frustrated sigh. "Just tell me why you decided to come back for me. Why now, when you didn't care what happened to me before?"

"If it wasn't now, I would have been too late," he whispered. He extended his hand, brushing his fingers over my cheek. His words and his touch were all I needed. I understood, and I didn't need to ask anything more.

I watched as he put the car in drive and he repeated, "Where to? "

Chapter Twenty-Four

It was sunset when we finally headed back to my house. After a few hours' worth of a drive, I told him to turn around; to go back to Point Judith. I couldn't stay in hiding, and I couldn't live in cold, wet, sandy clothes with no money and no paints. Hades gave me a questioning glance, "Are you sure?"

I gave him a quick, curt nod. I didn't know what it was that made me want to turn around and go home. It could have been the simple truth that I knew there was no place to run and hide. Not even in the Underworld. Someone could always come down and tell me I had to go back to her. I didn't want that. I wanted to be free. I wanted to be with him, even if it were only moments in the car, silent and foreboding. He didn't ask for directions on how to get back to my house. It seemed as if he had been there so many times that he knew it by memory. He pulled into the rocky driveway. The house loomed over us.

Things were darker; the air even seemed thicker than usual. As I got out of the car, I glanced around, hoping to notice her out on the beach or something, but everything was quiet. The only sounds were the waves crashing in our backyard. I felt him grab my hand suddenly, and he looked at me.

"I don't want to make some scene here with you, Summer," he said shaking his head. "I don't want to stand here and say that I love you or that I made a huge mistake in letting you go." I stood still, eyeing his fingers on mine. "I just want you to know that I'm not going to give up so easily."

I didn't reply. I didn't want to play along as the forgiving heroine who threw her arms around her hero. It wasn't us. I gave him another nod, and he seemed content with it. I understood what he was trying to say. I understood that so many things were about to, or could, happen, and there was a chance that I would die, or be reincarnated into someone else. Someone who wouldn't remember any of this. Wouldn't remember Hades. He gently squeezed my hand and allowed me to go in first. That was the plan.

I opened the front door and entered the living room, taking in the emptiness of the room. Our sofa was covered in sheets while all of my paintings were gone. My house was only a shell of what it once had been. It had been a great cover up to a great lie. I turned my head at the sound of the door closing and saw him standing there silently, watching. He was all eyes and all ears for me. I moved to the dark kitchen and reached out blindly for the table. I felt his hands on mine instantly, guiding my hands to the table. As soon as I was stable and had my footing, I looked up at him blindly, trying to make out his face in the dark.

"I think she might be outside," I whispered softly.

I heard Hades let out a soft noise; I wasn't sure if he was agreeing or not, but I watched him move to the back door, a slinky long shadow with no beginning and no end.

"Yes, she's out there. She's waiting," he murmured, and I bit down on my lower lip nervously.

"You don't have to do this," he said, but I quickly shook my head despite the fact that he couldn't see me.

"No," I managed. "No, I need to do this. I need to stop being so afraid."

"I'll be right behind you," he said in reply. I heard the back door open, and a stream of dim moonlight hit the floor, illuminating the kitchen. I didn't realize what I was doing until I was half way out the door.

I saw her standing near the waves, the little jar behind her in the dry sand. I wondered what would happen if I ran up and stole it and destroyed it. I glanced back at Hades in the darkness, and he gestured for me to go on. I moved. I walked toward her. She didn't realize I was there until I was nearly on top of her.

"I knew you'd come back."

"You're right about everything," I whispered. Her expression changed, and she seemed pleased with my revelation, even if it was false. "You're right. We belong together," I sighed, "Mother." It was all I could do to answer to her with that name. It was strange to think that she had always been mother to me, and now she was a woman I hated. She was a woman who had lied to me.

Her face seemed happy, relieved. "I knew you'd come to understand. I knew…" she stopped as her gaze moved over my shoulder to the shadow that I felt was there, watching.

"Why is he here?" She looked at me, startled and angry. I smirked a little, feeling strong; powerful even. "I don't understand this, Summer. I thought"— her eyes darted to the jar the same time mine had. She seemed to have read my mind. In an instant, the both of us were running, pushing at each other, screaming. I reached for it first, touching it with my finger, while with my other arm, shoved her away. Once I had it in my grasp, I ran to Hades.

"This is over!" I shouted. "I won't let you use me anymore." I watched as she pushed her blonde hair out of her face as she glared at me.

"You don't even understand what you're talking about." She sneered.

"I know everything," I said, letting tears fill my eyes. I had come so far. From the first moment that I had seen Hades on this very beach, to the moment of the car accident; my father's eyes on me through the rearview mirror, my mother's laughter. It was so distant, so long ago. And him. Him rescuing me from the hospital. His soft touches, his urgency to protect me. I turned to him, giving him the jar.

"She belongs to you," I said and watched as he went from looking confused to knowing.

"You never loved her," I heard Demeter scream.

Hades lifted his gaze and shook his head. "You are a stupid woman, Demeter. Stupid. Wait until everyone hears about what you've done to your daughters."

"No one will hear about it," she said, her lips twisting in rage. She began to walk toward him, holding out her hands for the jar.

"You give her back. All of her. Every bit of her," she said through clenched teeth.

Hades took a step back and shook his head. I stepped in between them, holding out my hands on either side. Hades shoved the jar back into my arms, and walked towards Demeter, reaching his hands out for her. I watched as his fingers wrapped around her neck.

"You killed her; you bitch. You killed her," he gasped with anger. "We had a deal, and you broke it. You are good for nothing. You deserve to die the way you killed her!"

I could hear her gasping, her body reaching for air. I watched it twist like a sculpture, twisting and turning for life that he was squeezing out of her. He shook her, pushing her back towards the ocean. I saw her glance over his shoulder, her eyes on me. Watching me as I stood and watched him kill her. I knew that I couldn't step in. I wouldn't stop him. He slowly began to release her body and lower her to the sand and the foam of the water. I knew then she was dead.

Slowly, he turned back toward me. "It's done now," he whispered. "We're done now." He stood there for a while, motionless, watching her body drift with the waves until she began to float into the deeper waters, churning with the white and blue, rocks and sand, becoming a part of the earth. I felt my legs slowly walk towards him, my hands touching his shoulders, his arms, and finally his hands that he held out in front of him. I saw his eyes slowly look into mine.

"Please forgive me, Summer," he said.

I didn't react. I didn't say a word. I took his face in my hands and slowly brought his lips down to mine. His lips were soft and warm and salty from the ocean. I felt his hands wrap around my body, and he held me close to him; his fingers grazed through my hair and down my neck. I could feel my body turning alive again, and I slowly pushed him away, biting my bottom lip; wanting to keep the imprint of his on mine forever.

"I'm sorry," he said, bowing his head.

"What now?" I managed after letting out a deep breath. His eyes fell back on the ocean, and then back to me.

"You could stay here," he said, lifting his hands to gesture to the house and the beach. This was where I wanted to be the whole time until I was away from him. I didn't know how to say what I wanted to say. I wanted to stay with him. I wanted to follow him; to go back to Greece, and into the caverns. I wanted him to be my home again.

"And I could come see you once in a while if you'd like," he said, shrugging a little. This was different. It was completely different from our first interaction with his promise to take me away. Now, things were different.

"Remember when," I began. "Remember when you said to me in the hospital that I still had a home with you?" I watched his eyes slowly rise up to meet mine. I knew he remembered. He silently nodded.

"Do you think," I bit my bottom lip nervously and pushed my hair out of my face. "Do you think I could come with you?"

"Is that what you really want?" he asked me, his lips turning into a slow smirk. I licked my lips and shook my head, letting out a soft laugh. "Do you really want me to say it?"

"Didn't I always?" he said with a chuckle and grabbed me, gently kissing me again. I wrapped my arms around his neck and managed to pull away for a breath.

"Let me come with you."

"I was going to drag you with me anyway," he said in a teasing tone.

"You won't be a jerk again?" I said with a laugh. He shrugged.

"No promises."

"What about art school?" I said, hopeful. "Can I still pursue my passion?"

"By all means. We can even live in a house like a real couple if you'd like," he said with a laugh.

"As long as I get to be with you." I nodded and lowered my forehead against his.

"I promise," I whispered. "I'll even eat pomegranate seeds if you'd like." I felt him chuckle against me more, and he slowly pulled me towards the house.

"I don't need you to do that, Summer. I need you to be yourself." I felt a sort of relief wash over me, and I grabbed his hand, holding it tightly. I knew in a matter of minutes; we'd be in the car, heading back to the airport, back to Greece; back to my home with him, happy forever.

Acknowledgements

First, I just want to say that I can't believe I'm actually here, to this point in my life. This has been a dream come true, and as I said to someone recently, Walt Disney was right. If you can dream it, you can do it.

Thank you to everyone who has ever helped me in this step: My parents, both who suffered a great deal with the loss of paper in the house when I was a teenager, and the money spent on notebook, after notebook as I wrote story after story. Mom, thank you for introducing me to books and the wonders that they hold. I know that without that experience, I wouldn't have loved to read or write as much as I do. Dad, for always cheering me on, encouraging me to keep following my dreams, and for being the best man in my whole life. (Me or Be?) My sister, who has always been there for me for everything. Without you, Carrine, my world wouldn't be this amazing or sweet. You are the greatest thing that's ever happened to me, and I hope you never, for a single second, forget that.

Roberto, without you, this novel wouldn't have been written. The endless nights of you reading and editing, re-reading, and editing, listening to me banter on and on about Greek Mythology and Hades, and always encouraging me to keep going -- to keep dreaming did not go unrecognized. I'm so glad that this book is something that I can share with you, among the many other things we share: I love you. To Shayne Leighton, who, read this book, told me to do something with it, and guided me to this point; this book wouldn't be finished without you.

A big thank you to Waldorf Publishing for saying yes to me. For all the help and support: without every single one of you, this book would not be here. For all of those who I have not thanked, or acknowledged, please know that my thanks go to you all whole heartily.

Author Bio

Chantal Gadoury is a young author who currently lives in Delaware, though originally from Muncy PA, with her two cats, Theo and Harper, and her fiancé Robert.

Chantal enjoys painting, drinking a good cup of coffee when she can and enjoys her favorite Disney classics. When she's not busy crafting or reading, Chantal is dedicated to her family: A mother, sister and a furry-puppy-brother (and sends a prayer to her father, who now resides in heaven.)

As a 2011 college graduate from Susquehanna University, with a degree in Creative Writing, 'Seven Seeds of Summer' is her first book, with a new novel to follow soon.